Also by Daniel Pinkwater

CHICAGO DAYS, HOBOKEN NIGHTS

FISH WHISTLE

THE AFTERLIFE DIET

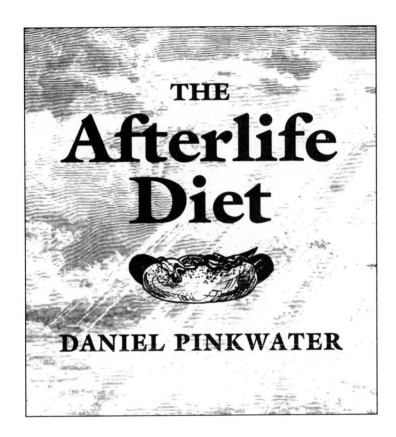

THE
Afterlife
Diet

DANIEL PINKWATER

Random House New York

Library of Congress Cataloging-in-Publication Data
Pinkwater, Daniel
The afterlife diet/Daniel Pinkwater.—1st ed.
p. cm.
ISBN 0-679-41936-5
I. Title.
PS3566.I526A69   1995
813'.54—dc20   94-21540

Manufactured in the United States of America
24689753
First Edition

Book Design and Illustration by Lilly Langotsky

For Jill

THE AFTERLIFE DIET

1

Milton Cramer, the lousy editor, woke up in a room he'd never seen before. He clearly remembered having died on the operating table at St. Agatha's Hospital in Potlatch, New York. There had been the classic out-of-body stuff, the dispassionate floating over the scene in the O.R. (attempts to resuscitate him hadn't been all that energetic, he thought), and the trip through the long tunnel toward the bright light.

According to a magazine article he'd once read, the next event would be his father, Ignatz, and his brothers, Moshie and Irving, all of whom had gone before, beckoning to him. This did not happen, which was all right with Milton. There would be plenty of time to look them up later, he thought. He had enough to handle without aggravation from family.

Instead of a reunion with his ancestors, Milton was met at the bright end by an enormous woman, a lot like the emergency-room nurse at the hospital, who conducted a curt interview with him. He couldn't remember the questions; it was unlikely they were about insurance. Then there was blackness—until now.

Milton remembered what he remembered perfectly well, but now he was busy denying it. He was trying to focus on what would no doubt turn out to be the recovery room, or his room on one of the floors in the hospital. There was no evidence of medical apparatus that Milton could see by rolling his eyes around. He hadn't moved a muscle thus far, waiting to figure out, as patients do, how injured he might be, what parts could move, and what tubes and catheters might be connected to him. What he was able to take in with eyeballs alone suggested a cheap, old, and run-down motel room.

When he discovered he could turn his head, he did so, and saw another bed beside the one he was in. On the bed was an enormous figure in graying underwear—a preposterously fat man, awake, gazing at the ceiling. Somehow the sight of the whale-like individual in the next bed had put an end to Milton's attempt to hope that he was experiencing, or remembering, weird hallucinations while coming out of anesthesia.

Milton propped himself up on his elbows, and over his belly, which was, if anything, bigger than the other man's, had a better look at the room. This was no hospital. It was also no hotel he'd have voluntarily checked into. The room was of a category beyond nondescript. If he had closed his eyes, he wouldn't have been able to remember what color the walls were.

The fat man in his underwear had not acknowledged him.

Milton spoke, "I'm Milton Cramer."

"Wonderful," the man on the other bed said, waspishly. "Who gives a fuck?"

"Mind telling me where I am?" Milton asked.

"Spare me," the other fat man said. "You know very well where you are." He hauled himself off the bed, pulled on a pair of royal blue sweatpants, and went to the door in his bare feet. He opened the door and said over his shoulder, "The can's down the hall. Bet you didn't think you'd need one here. Welcome to the Happy Hunting Ground." He padded away, leaving the door half-open.

"I didn't think anything," Milton thought. "I wasn't counting on any of this. Only last night I was busy getting murdered."

Milton found that it made him queasy to remember the events leading up to his departure from St. Agatha's. He tried to shake off the images. It occurred to him that he too could get out of bed. The last time he'd seen himself, from just under the rafters of the operating room, he'd had an incision in his monumental belly suggestive of the opening of a gladstone bag. He tentatively felt his paunch. It was whole and spherical. He swung his legs over the side of the bed, and stood up. Everything normal. He was naked. Hanging on a hook, he found a pair of gym shorts, and a T-shirt inscribed with the name of an alma mater of his, "Camp Yiddishe Kinder of the Berkshires." He'd had a shirt like this—or this shirt—only it was now triple-extra-large, like the shorts. The pair of Nike sneakers he recognized as his very own, purchased not three years earlier and still in good shape, as he had hardly walked in them. He dressed and went outside.

"I have died and gone to Heaven," Milton thought, "and Heaven is a resort in the Catskills."

Dimly, he remembered Ignatz and Martha had taken

their three sons, Milton, the youngest, hardly more than a baby, to a place like this. There was the "Manor," an old frame farm structure, converted and expanded over years to house more guests. Surrounding it, buildings, of graduated size, reflecting the resort's growth—the older, smaller ones barracks-like, and the newest suggesting transplanted apartment houses from Queens and Riverdale. Everything was painted white and ghastly aquamarine. There was the "Casino," where nightly entertainments were held. There were the lawn chairs, the outdoor card tables, the flower beds, the concrete fountain with no water running—and the guests, in the lawn chairs, sleeping with heads thrown back, sitting in groups, talking, and not talking, playing dominoes, waiting for the next meal. Others were strolling, promenading, or merely standing. A few were playing shuffleboard, or whacking tennis balls on a cracked and weedy court. Every one of them was fat!

"Are we settling in nicely?" Except one. A trim, middle-aged man in a costume suitable for gymnastics, loose purple trousers and a sleeveless athletic shirt, had bounded up to Milton from behind. "I'm Charlie. They have me doing everything around here. Jack of all trades, and master of none, you know? Any questions . . . you ask me."

Milton had a lot of questions, but Charlie, who had been bouncing on the balls of his feet, and shuffling from side to side like a shadowboxer during the whole ten seconds he'd been speaking, was now moving down the path, jogging backward.

"Breakfast in twenty minutes," he said, as the distance between them increased. "The headwaiter will show you to your assigned seat. His name is André. Slip him a finif, and he'll take care of you. He's my son, the little bastard, so I know he needs the dough. We'll talk later."

Charlie was fifty feet away by now. He flitted out of sight, pumping his arms and sucking in deep breaths.

It wasn't hard to find the dining room. It was in a 1960s-modern structure with a sizable knot of what Milton could only assume were fellow deceased, all of them markedly circumferentially challenged, standing around and eyeing the locked doors.

Milton spied his roommate, chatting amiably with a blond woman who resembled a Volkswagen in a yellow muumuu.

"There he is now," the roommate said. "My bunkie."

Milton approached them. "Look," he said.

"Yes?"

"Is anyone going to tell me what goes on around here?"

"What goes on around here is what goes on around here. It's completely obvious. New arrivals are such a pain in the ass, with all the questions. By the way, I am Otto Von Hinten, and this is Angela Podgorny."

"Pleased to make your acquaintance," the woman in the muumuu said. She was about four foot nine. "Otto is annoyed because they put you in his room. He was promised a single."

"I'd prefer a single myself," Milton said. "Who do I talk to?"

"You could talk to Charlie. Have you met Charlie?" Angela asked.

"Just now. He told me to give five dollars to the head-waiter, but does anybody have any money here?"

"Of course not," Otto Von Hinten said. "This is the realm of the dead. Charlie is always pretending to look for a shmear, which gives him an excuse for doing nothing, since nobody here has a nickel. He told me that for twenty-five he would get me a single room in one of the new buildings."

"So you don't like it here," Milton said.

"The food isn't bad," Otto said. "And there are some good chess players. If I could get a nice room, with an air conditioner . . . but it's next to impossible. Think about it. Nobody leaves. Nobody moves. Nobody dies. I'm going to be stuck with you in that crummy room for eternity. Get it? Eternity."

"And the ones who have the nice rooms?"

"They died first. There are people who have been here since Buddha was a pup. The place is getting full, but do they come in and remodel, or put up a new building? Another thing . . . wait until you see what sort of movies we get. I mean, wouldn't you think we'd have first-run movies? Last week was *The Sound of Music*. I ask you."

"And you've seen the condition of the tennis courts?" Angela Podgorny said. "I've spoken to Charlie, I don't know how many times. . . . Look! The dining room is open. Come sit with us."

"I thought it was assigned seating," Milton said.

"Assigned seating! Nobody cares," Otto said. "For a month we haven't had prunes. No prunes. Can you believe it? There are a lot of old people here. Does anybody give a damn? You arrived here too late, my friend. This place is going to hell."

"Unless it *is* Hell," Milton said.

"Ha! In Hell they have prunes."

The dining room filled up in five minutes. Waiters, none of them fat, circulated efficiently and kept up with the residents, who addressed their breakfasts with energy. There was a low murmur beneath the noises of crockery and utensils. Milton assumed that the conversation at the other tables was similar to what was being said at his.

"Do we have any of the pineapple Danishes?"

"How's the lox omelet?"

"I wanted whole wheat."

"Could you pass the syrup?"

"What is that, blueberry?"

"I need milk for my coffee."

"Fresh fruit. Fresh fruit is all I eat in the morning."

"Ketchup on eggs? Who puts ketchup on eggs?"

"Taste this. They put lemon and powdered sugar on it."

"Don't touch the sausages. They could kill you, ha ha."

In addition to Otto and Angela, there were five others at the table. No names were exchanged. Milton tried a number of times to ask the many questions that were on his mind. There was no response. The table talk was strictly focused on what was on the table. When the others were finished feeding, they rose and departed without a word.

At the end, it was Milton and Angela. "Please . . . I'm in agony. Won't anybody explain things to me?"

"Look, dear," Angela said. "It's just too tedious and painful to go over and over the details. When you've been here awhile, you'll understand. It's so much better just to concentrate on the here and now. Everybody who comes here has the same questions, thousands of them, and they want to ask them over and over. It doesn't matter how carefully we would explain—they would still ask again and again. And it would never end. Fat people die every day."

"Why fat people?" Milton asked.

"Because that's who comes here," Angela said. "You see? You're doing it still. Look around. Do you really need to ask? And yet you ask. And you'll ask more."

"Only fat people? Where are the others?"

"I'm going to take a nap, darling," Angela said.

"Maybe later we can play shuffleboard. Try to stop asking—you'll make friends better."

Angela dabbed at her lips with a napkin, and rose from her chair. She patted Milton's arm. "At night, go to the casino. That's the best thing. Soon you'll be comfortable." Few of the residents remained in the dining room. The cleanup crew was noisily clearing plates. Milton went outside, and decided to walk around and reconnoiter. The place was vast. Beyond the central complex of buildings were meadows and forests, with endless gravel paths. There were pleasant views of mountains and lakes. It was pretty, all right. A good enough sort of heaven, Milton thought, for some.

Milton found a barn and a corral, containing a dozen horses. He leaned on a fence rail, and a palomino mare ambled over to him and nuzzled his hand. He hadn't had much to do with horses, but he felt a surge of emotion at the display of affection. He stroked the mare's muzzle for a time. It soothed him.

He became aware of a woman doing the same thing, vis-à-vis a chestnut gelding at the angle of the fence. She appeared to be in her thirties, and had a nice figure in a Venus-of-Willendorf sort of way. Milton walked over.

"You like horses?" he asked. He had figured out that anything but small talk resulted in a stone-wall response from the inmates.

"You're a new arrival, and you're trying to shmooze your way up to asking me the usual questions," the woman said.

"That's right," Milton said.

"Take your best shot," the woman said. "I used to be a social worker. If it gets too obnoxious, you agree to quit, all right?"

"It's a deal," Milton said. "Thanks."

"OK. Yes, I like horses. My name's Natalie. Next question, please."

"It's been a hell of a morning," Milton said. "I'm all confused."

"Well, it's a big change."

Milton's mind was racing. He found he couldn't say anything. He was trying to formulate his questions in such a way that he would have gotten the maximum of information by the time Natalie decided it was too boring or annoying to go on answering. At the same time he was automatically sizing her up. She wore white tennis shorts and a T-shirt. Her hair was light brown, streaked with gray. She was tanned and healthy-looking, with clear blue eyes.

"As long as you're staring at my breasts, I'll cover an easy one first," she said. "Yes, we are able to have sex— but just about nobody does."

"Why not?" Milton asked.

"Because it's perfect here. No matter how great it was for you in the world of the living . . ."

"It was never all that great for me," Milton said, and realized.

". . . here, it is perfect to a degree you could never have imagined. As a result of which, after you've done it once or possibly twice, you just never feel like doing it again. It's one of those once-in-a-deathtime things."

"Interesting," Milton said. "All of a sudden I comprehend that what makes being alive interesting is all the imperfection, and the persistent desire to make things better."

"You're catching on. Did you have breakfast?"

"I nibbled a little."

"And how did you like the cooking?"

"It . . . couldn't have been better," Milton said.

"And how do you feel, physically?"

"Perfect."

"You get the picture? The things that motivated you in the other place don't apply here."

"But how about the crummy room I woke up in?" Milton asked. "My roommate, Otto, does nothing but complain. In fact, all I've heard anybody do today is kvetch about the facilities, and how new arrivals ask boring questions."

"Think about it," Natalie said. "How could all the whinging and whining be consistent with perfection?"

Milton thought. "It's consistent with a place like this for the guests to complain all the time?"

"And have something to complain about," Natalie said. "Even though most people here try to give the impression that they're old hands at being dead, they're still attached to the processes of being alive. It's awesome and uncomfortable to deal with experience that isn't vitiated by the half-assed quality of life, as it is lived by the living."

"So the flaws are built in to give us a sense of normalcy," Milton said.

"Such is my belief," Natalie said.

"Then personal progress is possible, even here," Milton said.

"Takes awhile," Natalie said.

"And presumably, one can arrive at a point where one is able to accept perfection, and not need to crap it up so that it resembles what we remember as normal human life. One could then, for example, take pleasure in sex."

"I will have to keep an eye on you," Natalie said.

"Been dead long?"

"Oh, a long time." She gave him a significant smile.

"Who is Charlie?" Milton asked.

"An angel, I guess," Natalie said. "Or something of the kind. The whole staff, the waiters and busboys, and maids too. They haven't been in the realm we come from."

"And why does everyone appear fat?" Milton asked.

"We *are* fat," Natalie said. "We were fat, and we continue to be fat."

"Only fat people get an afterlife?"

"Only fat people get *this* afterlife."

"Where are the others?" Milton asked.

"Well, of course, no one knows for sure," Natalie said. "The general belief is that the thin ones have a place of their own—much nicer. I've heard it said that they have color TV in the rooms, a heated indoor pool, and a Thai restaurant. Also a really fantastic golf course. And they go on bus trips."

"Why isn't everybody together?" Milton asked.

"They don't like to look at us. We're a blot on the landscape."

"What? They're snobs?"

"We make them uncomfortable. You know how most people are. They'd rather be dead than fat."

Milton and Natalie were leaning against the corral fence. The midmorning sun warmed them. The horses had fallen asleep, standing with one hind foot cocked. A soft breeze came up. A dragonfly buzzed.

Milton had suddenly run out of questions. His mind shut down. He entered into the stillness, and stayed there for he knew not how long. Natalie seemed to be occupying the same pleasant mental void.

When Milton was returned to himself, it was as if he was waking from a long sleep. He experienced something like a volume knob turned up from zero to a level at which he could hear the insect noises and birdsongs, and the horses' breathing.

"Very peaceful," he said.

"As advertised," Natalie said.

Their voices sounded hollow to Milton after the long pause.

"I can't think of anything more to ask. . . ."

"You have a lot to absorb."

". . . I mean, there's a lot I want to know, but I can't seem to formulate a question."

"Perfectly all right. There's no hurry."

"Shall we take a walk?" Milton asked.

"Not at this time," Natalie said. "I think I'll go to my room and lie down. Please don't take it personally, but you give me a terrific headache."

"Of course. No offense taken."

"It's not you—it's the condition of your inner being. When people first come here, they have this . . . it's like the smell of the other world, and . . . well, they tend to be something of a strain on us old-timers."

"A smell? Like sewer gas, you mean?"

Natalie gave Milton a kiss. Its amorous content was well below 25 percent, but it still surpassed all the combined instances of passion he'd ever known, also all music, art, World Series games, pizzas, and horse races.

Milton was struck mute.

"Go to the casino in the evening," Natalie said. "That's where you'll get your answers." She started up the path. "See you around."

Milton said nothing.

That night, after leaving the dining room (Milton had not only paid attention to the food, but had put away substantial quantities of brisket that was literally to die for), he wandered into the basilica-shaped stucco building with the blue neon CASINO sign, surrounded by a swarm of mosquitoes. It was the classic gymnasium *cum* auditorium, as found in schools and camps. There was a small, simple stage at one end, and rows of folding chairs, about half of which creaked under the weight of extinct endomorphs.

Presently, Charlie appeared, wearing a tuxedo jacket with sequined lapels.

"Hey, good evening, ladies and ghosts! Welcome, welcome to the casino! I'm Charlie, your master of cemeteries, uh, ceremonies. We have a wonderful evening planned for your entertainment, so look alive, everybody . . . or, if you can't manage it, look dead in a pleasant way.

"This fat lady comes up to me and says, 'I'm too heavy, and my hair looks terrible.'

" 'So, diet,' I tell her.

" 'I'm going to, but I can't decide what color.'

"Hey!

"I know a guy who's so fat . . ."

"How fat is he?" the audience shouted.

". . . he had the mumps two weeks before he knew it.

"Ba-dum!

"He was so fat he was arrested for jaywalking, and all the time, he was waiting on the corner for the light to change.

"Zetz!

"I know a woman who's so fat, every time she falls down, she rocks herself to sleep.

"She had to give up golf, because when she puts the ball where she can see it, she can't hit it . . ."

"And when she puts the ball where she can hit it, she can't see it!" someone in the audience shouted.

"Uh-oh, someone's been putting Benzedrine in his Ovaltine," Charlie quipped, pointing at the man who had spoken. The departed clapped and roared approval.

Charlie crouched at the edge of the stage, concentrating on the heckler.

"At least he's not overweight—just six inches too short.

"Nice suit, pal. I heard you got it for a ridiculous figure.

"I'm just kidding. He's a nice guy. Went to church three times in his life. The first time they threw water on him, the second time they threw rice on him, the third time they threw dirt on him.

"He used to exercise with dumbbells, but they got wise.

"Hey!

"Zetz!

"Are we having fun, or what!"

Incredibly, to Milton, the others *were* having fun. He wasn't. His jaw had dropped several stale gags earlier, and remained so.

"No, no. You know I love you all," Charlie was saying. "I insult you, and call you fat pigs, and chubby, gross, disgusting, obese gluttons and tubs of lard—but I do it with love."

There was a round of applause, and Charlie dabbed at his eyes with a handkerchief.

"Thank you, thank you, ladies and elephants."

Milton had had all he could take. He began to rise from his seat, with the intention of going out the door.

"But now, what you *really* came to see," Charlie said. "A really class act. Everybody's favorite deity. A real professional. The big guy. The boss. Let's give a big hand to the Great Life Force, the Invisible Principle, the Tao, Logos. Ladies and gentlemen, it's my privilege to introduce God the Father! Give it up for God, now!"

Thunderous handclapping. Milton sank onto his chair. Charlie pranced off the stage sideways, one hand extended in a gesture of presentation.

The stage was bathed in dazzling light, which became brighter and brighter, until the whole far end of the casino was one coruscating whiteness. Milton was losing all physical sensation. He was no longer aware of the others in the audience. He had no hands to clap, no feet to rest on the floor, no buttocks to sit on the chair, no floor, no chair, no eyes, no ears, no brain, no memory, no identity, and no absence of memory, no absence of identity, no nothing, or almost no nothing.

A voice that could only have been God's voice said, "I just flew in from the coast, and boy, are My arms tired. . . ." at which point, Milton's last vestige of anything like consciousness disappeared, and he was subsumed into the brightness.

3

Dr. Alan Plotkin speared a pickle slice from the stainless steel tub on the table and munched it contemplatively. An identical tub contained a few shreds of coleslaw.

"Joe, some more slaw here!" the enormous psychotherapist called. To the fat individual sitting across from him, Plotkin said, "Have a knish, Milo."

"I couldn't eat another thing, Doctor," Milo said. Milo's girth would have been impressive in any other company. Contrasted to Plotkin's mountainous expanse, swathed in charcoal pinstripe, he appeared merely chubby. Plotkin gave the impression of being seated on two chairs. His huge hands were in constant easy and graceful motion conveying pickle slices, crusts of rye bread, shreds of pastrami to his mouth.

"We have a few minutes left, Milo. You want some more coffee—a blueberry muffin? Joe! Bring Milo a blueberry muffin!"

"You finished them, Doc. He want a cruller?"

"You want a cruller?"

"Yeah. A cruller, Joe!"

"That OK, Doc?"

"Yeah. Bring him a cruller—and one for me!"

The Korean proprietor brought crullers and poured coffee. The two men chewed in silence.

"So tell me more about your stepfather."

"He won't let me live."

"What do you mean by that? Gimme the cream."

"He's on my case all the time. He won't let me leave the business, and he won't let me work."

"Give an example."

"OK. We got this shipment of Double Yellowheads. Fifteen of them, from a breeder in Wisconsin. We've gotten from him before. Well, the birds arrived in really awful condition."

"Like what? Sour crop? Diarrhea? Scaly feet?"

"Some of that, and just scuzzy. Dull, matted feathers, skin problems, parasites. They were a mess."

"And?"

"So I wanted to refuse the shipment. Send the birds back. The old man says no, I have to stay there most of the night doctoring the damn parrots."

"What'd you give 'em, a broad-spectrum antibiotic?"

"Psittacyclene, and I had to spray 'em and shmear their feet, and shove vitamins down 'em, and then hang around and watch 'em to see none of them reacted. I was there till ten o'clock. And I was supposed to see Gloria."

"How is it going with Gloria?"

"She won't listen to reason."

"Still claims she loves you, but won't go out with you?"

"I told her I like her fat. I prefer her fat. If she wasn't having a good time with me she wouldn't have gained that forty-five pounds. With me she could let herself go."

"And she says?"

"She doesn't want to let herself go. She says she doesn't want to weigh a hundred and eighty-seven."

"That's not heavy for a girl."

"I tell her that. She doesn't want to hear it. Anyway, I persuaded her to meet me at a Turkish restaurant I read about. I had to bend the gates of Hell to get her to agree. She was already moaning that I was going to make her pig out on baklava and then take her home to bed—and I would have, too, except I wound up nursing all those goddamn parrots far into the night. When I finally got done and called her she'd left a message on her machine that she had gone to an Overeaters Anonymous meeting."

"And you couldn't tell your stepfather no?"

"Sure. Remember what he did the time I tried that?"

"Yes. Well, you have a point."

"Yes."

"So, how's the writing going?" Plotkin asked, running his finger around his plate, picking up crumbs.

"I don't know. I can't seem to get anything started," Milo said. "I keep waiting to hear about the book."

"You sent it to publishers?"

"I sent it to a lot of publishers. I spent over five hundred dollars on Xeroxing and postage."

"And?"

"So far, I've gotten thirty-three form letters, rejecting it. Not all the copies of the manuscript have come back, but not one of the ones that have has been read. After the first dozen rejections, I figured out this trick—I put a couple of thin threads of rubber cement along the edge of the pages, barely noticeable. But if you read it, the threads will be broken."

"And the threads aren't broken?"

"On a couple of them, it looks like someone may have looked at the first couple of pages."

"Must be depressing," Plotkin said, licking his finger.

"You have to know somebody, Doc," Milo said. "Sending stuff in cold is a waste of time. So far, I've only gotten one letter from an actual person—some guy named Cramer at Harlon House."

"What did he say?"

"Almost the same as the form letters. It's not right for their list, and good luck. Only this Cramer guy said he might be interested in having me write something for one of their series."

"Well, isn't that a possibility?" Plotkin asked.

"I don't know," Milo said. "When I took the course in how to get published, the professor told us about these cheap publishers that crank out romance novels and westerns. They pay a flat fee, and keep all the profits, and the stuff they have you write is crap. They give you guidelines—all the books have to be the same. He mentioned Harlon House, specifically, as an example of the kind of place to stay away from."

"So why'd you submit your book to them in the first place?"

"I don't know, except I was running out of publishers. I was just about sure they wouldn't be interested in a novel like mine."

"It's *Moby-Dick,* told from the point of view of the whale, isn't that right?"

"Yes. You didn't read the copy I gave you?"

"I'm saving it for my vacation," Plotkin said. "I've got

a heavy caseload. So, are you going to call this guy at Harlon House?"

"You think I should?"

"What have you got to lose? Listen to what he has to say. Maybe you could make some contacts, and if you decide to write something for them, get some experience—they must pay something."

"True. I could recoup what I spent sending *Call Me Whale* around, with a little left over. I'll think it over."

"OK, Milo, that's all the time we have today. I'll see you tomorrow."

"OK, Doctor."

Milo took the green slip of paper to the cash register. Joe mumbled the total, "Lessee, you had four pastramis, fries, four sodas, coffee, the crullers, with the therapy comes to a hundred and twenty-nine eighty." Milo made out a check to Psycho-Deli Associates. He paused in the doorway. "OK, I'll see you tomorrow, Doctor."

"OK, Milo! Joe, send over my next client, and a Linzer tart!"

Bird Wirld occupied a shabby brick warehouse building on Sedgewick Street. The windows were dark and grimy. Nothing about the building invited access. The door was a scuffed and dented metal one, over which was a small hand lettered sign—white letters on a blackened board: BIRD RING BELL.

In these unpromising premises, Felix MacGregor conducted a unique enterprise in avian exotica. No one, least of all Milo, who was now scalding cages while Count Rothschild and Captain Dreyfuss, two magnificent African Greys, personal pets of MacGregor, hopped and fluttered around the messy stockroom, knew for how many millions the business accounted. This much was known, it was by far the largest undertaking of its kind—it was international in scope—and Felix's was the last word in the parrot trade. It was generally understood that MacGregor was not his original name.

"You like dis, boid?" Felix MacGregor said to the Scarlet Macaw with which he was eating slices of avocado. "You like dis, little Pierre Mendez-France?"

The macaw, an enormous variegated thing, gnawed on the piece of avocado it held in its scaly claw, cocked its head, and made a noise like a rusty hinge.

"Ah, good boid!" Felix said. Milo, stepson of Felix, entered the office. "Bummer!" he shouted. "Bummer! Loafer! Idiot! You hed lunch vit your friend, the fet vitch doctor already? You left another hundred dollars for pastrami and Jewish Christian Science? Your complexes are better now, schlemiel? So go clean out the cages frum Count Rothschild and Captain Dreyfuss, you elephant, before I give you that you vouldn't know where it came from."

"I just did that," Milo said. "And you'd like me better if I *were* an elephant."

"You *are* an elephant, I still don't like you." To the bird, "Come, Mendez-France, bubbaleh—eat avocado vit Felix."

Milo owned a bird of the parrot family himself—a small green parakeet named Marcel Proust. The bird had a neurotic habit of plucking out its tail feathers, giving itself a stumpy and ungainly appearance.

MacGregor returned Mendez-France to his cage. "Hey, slob!" he called to Milo. "I vant you should help Rubinstein."

"Your friend Rubinstein, the guy with the hot-dog stand?"

"No, helf-vit, Rubinstein the pianist—of course Rubinstein vit deh hot-dog stand. You'll help him."

"Help him with what?"

"Vit vhatever he vants you should help him, you miserable yutz! Go already to Rubinstein's place. Maybe he can loin you something."

"What does he expect me to do? I don't know anything about the hot-dog business."

"You don't know anything pee-riod! Look, schmuck, Rubinstein needs somebody should help him in his voik. You'll help him, see?"

"Now?"

"What, next Hallowe'en? Yes, now, you ape!"

"But after I finish here I have to take those cockatiels to Pet City. Then I was going to work on my . . . on my . . ."

"And after det you'll disappear and go and schtup your fet girlfriend for a couple days, yes? I vill take the cockatiels. You vill help Rubinstein. Now go, imbecile!"

"This is just for today, right?"

"Dis is for until Rubinstein sends you beck, putz! Are you going or am I hitting?"

"Wait a minute, are you *giving* me to Rubinstein?"

"Who's giving? You'll help him."

"Who's going to pay for my time?"

"Your boss vill pay you."

"You're my boss."

"Rubinstein is your boss. Now go there before he dies already."

"You're firing me, is that it?" Milo hated working for his stepfather in the wholesale aviary business, and had tried to quit repeatedly—but Felix had never allowed it, and he had the trump card, influence with Milo's mother, Phyllis, who had influence over Milo. Now, Milo perceived, he was being delivered from bird-bondage, but into something probably as horrible, or more horrible, but anyway different.

"I'm not firing," Felix MacGregor said, in an almost kindly tone. "I'm . . . lending."

"I don't have anything to say about this?"

"Ouch is vhat you'll say if you don't get outta here, you bull moose."

Milo recognized from certain signs that Felix was about to become violent. He grabbed his coat and headed for the door.

"Listen vhat Rubinstein tells you!" his stepfather called after him.

5

"So, you were referred by . . . ?"

"Milo Levi-Nathan," Milton Cramer said. "One of our writers. I ran into him where he works—his day job—he's a counterman at Rubinstein's Orthodox Hot Dogs."

"I know it well," Alan Plotkin said. "They do a Polish like nobody does, with the spicy onions and the brown mustard."

"Don't remind me," Milton said. "I had six of them that night. Then I . . . I just lost it. . . . I was overcome with guilt. I stood there with a half-eaten sausage in my hand and cried like a baby."

"The human condition," Plotkin said. "So Milo comforted you?"

"Yes, he was very sympathetic. He told me about you."

"Milo is a good person." Plotkin made a note in his book: Free session for Levi-Nathan when Cramer comes three times.

"But, now that I'm here, I'm not sure you're the right therapist for me," Milton said.

"And why is that?"

"You're . . . quite large," Milton said.

"And that's a problem?"

"No, it's just . . . I had the impression you were helping Milo . . . uh . . . lose weight."

"Lose weight?"

"I just assumed. He said he was becoming much more comfortable with himself. He said you'd helped him."

"Lose weight?"

"Well, I thought . . ."

"Look, you can try to lose weight if you want—but it won't do you the least good. The problem isn't physical."

"It isn't?"

"We're going to do this the classical way," Plotkin said. "My assistant will help me push these tables together. Joe, setup for a deep regression, and then I want a baked apple."

Joe and Plotkin pushed three tables together, covered them with a crocheted afghan, and placed a pillow at one end.

"Just hop on here, and stretch out," Plotkin said.

"Here? In a luncheonette?"

"It's also a clinic," Plotkin said. "Get comfortable. You want something to nibble?"

"Maybe one of those big chocolate-chip cookies?"

"Good choice. Now let's get started," Plotkin said.

"What do I do?" Milton asked.

"Just go back as far as you can. Remember the earliest thing you can," Plotkin said. "Here's a napkin—you're getting crumbs on your sweater."

Milton closed his eyes. He took tiny bites from his

cookie, working all around the edges. Plotkin made a note.

"Ooo, I can remember the apartment we lived in when I was a little child."

"Uh-huh," Plotkin said.

"Aww, my little room, where I slept with my brothers, Moshie and Irving. So cute, with all the toys, and the model airplanes!"

"Mmmm?" said Plotkin. Without making a sound, Joe handed Plotkin his baked apple.

"I was happy then."

"You were?"

"Yes, I had a happy childhood. I loved my family, my parents and my brothers, and they loved me."

"That so?"

"Of course, Moshie and Irving weren't *always* nice to me," Milton said.

"Um," said Plotkin.

"Oh, not very often, but sometimes they picked on me."

"But not often?"

"No. Yes. Often. All the time. They laughed at me. They thought I was nothing but a joke."

"Whyzzat?" Plotkin asked.

"Because . . . because . . . Mommy and Daddy laughed at me. They *all* made fun of me!"

"Why?"

"Because I was stupid!"

"And were you stupid?"

Milton propped himself up on an elbow, and twisted to face Plotkin. "Well, yes, I was, compared to them. My father worked in the post office his whole life—his family was poor, it was the Depression, he couldn't go to college—but his hobby was neurology. He had hundreds of books, and model brains, and real brains, and charts of the nervous system, around the house. He used to astound doctors. My mother was an authority on Eastern European folk songs. And both my brothers became dermatologists. They specialized in nervous disorders of the skin. A lot of famous folksingers were their clients."

"Lie back. Close your eyes. Let's get back to remembering. Tell me, if you can, the first time you felt that your family thought you were stupid."

"Grapes," Milton said.

"Grapes? You want grapes?"

"I was eating grapes. I must have been three or four. I remember stuffing lots of grapes into my cheeks, like a chipmunk. I remember how it felt. The grapes were cool and leaked sweet juice. My brother Moshie laughed at me. He pointed. 'Look how stupid he looks!' he said. 'The fat little moron!' And Irving laughed, and Mommy and Daddy laughed. My father said, 'I'm afraid you're right. Milton will never make a dermatologist.' It was his dream that all his sons would be dermatologists."

"And how did you feel—at the time?"

"At the time, I just accepted it. I didn't feel insulted until just this minute. Up until now, when I remembered that exchange—if I ever remembered it—I just thought about the grapes. They were the seedless kind."

"Red or green?"

"Green," Milton said. Plotkin made a note. "Understand, my brothers were wonderful men, and we were very close. I still haven't gotten over their deaths, and the way they were killed."

"They were killed?"

"Mysteriously, in a grotesque and horrible way."

"Maybe we can start with that next time," Plotkin said.

"We're done?"

"Almost. Time flies."

"Yes, it does."

"He wanted you all to be dermatologists?"

"Yes. He said it was the easiest specialty."

"Except for one," Plotkin said. "Well, I think we've made a very promising start. Tell Joe to schedule you for another appointment Thursday or Friday. I think twice a week will do to begin with."

"That's it?" Milton asked.

"For now," Plotkin said.

6

Hugh Rubinstein was a snappy dresser to a stunning degree. Probably the last exponent of the modified zoot suit walking around loose, his attire was a derangement of fabrics in an unforeseen range of colors, weaves, and patterns. In addition, he adorned himself with numerous diamonds, in all of the usual places, and one in a tooth. Add to his fashion sense a maniacal cleanliness, and preoccupation with grooming—polished nails, polished shoes, dazzling linen, and everything pressed to knife-like sharpness—and the complete effect was of five feet, two inches of incandescent entrepreneur.

He was the owner of two cherished prizewinning Apricot-crested Cockatoos, supplied by Felix MacGregor, and operated the climax, crown, culmination, and epitome of hot-dog stands, Rubinstein's Orthodox Hot Dogs, known everywhere.

The original Rubinstein's had created a sensation when

it opened in Vienna in the last century, and Hugh's great-grandfather and grandfather were said to have delivered takeout to the Imperial Palace, and, it was further rumored, his grandmother, Grimna, a beauty in her day, had been sent for by way of an appetizer on more than one occasion. Hugh Rubinstein secretly suspected that he was partially of Hapsburg pedigree—but he knew for certain that hot dogs were in his blood.

"This is the steam table," he said to Milo Levi-Nathan on Milo's first day. "What the typewriter was to Faulkner and the piano was to Chopin, the steam table is to you. From this day forward, you are a hot-dog man. There is nothing finer. Congratulations."

Milo, in his starched white apron and crisp paper hat, flushed with pride. His co-workers, veteran hotdoggers, had the aspect of players on a world's championship sports team, or an élite guards unit. Half an hour before opening time, they stood casually at their posts, making ready, with an easy confidence, a relaxed athleticism. Their hands were steady, their eyes were clear. They appeared to glow with health, possibly because of their regular consumption of Rubinstein's product, advertised on a huge sign that arched over their heads: THE BEST FOOD ON EARTH.

"This is Linda," Rubinstein said. "Linda will teach you the ways of the hot dog. I leave you in her care."

Rubinstein departed for his office at the rear of the shop. The establishment was large, extending along two thirds of a city block, fully enclosed—glassed in, with able counterpersons stationed at intervals along its length.

"Welcome, Milo," Linda said, gripping his hand firmly with her plastic disposable glove. "The basic hot dog, Chicago-style. Watch me assemble one, and then we'll do one together, OK?"

Linda was an ample blonde, with cornflower eyes and pink skin that glistened with light perspiration. A wisp of gold peeked out from under the edge of her hairnet. She was slightly flushed, as though she herself has just come out of the steamer. "It's all beef," Linda lectured. "It's got a natural casing—it snaps when you bite into it, and squirts hot juice. And we never boil them."

"Never boil them," Milo repeated thickly.

"The water is between a hundred seventy and a hundred ninety Fahrenheit. See the thermometer? When they float to the surface, and redden slightly, we fish them out. See?" Milo felt himself redden slightly as Linda handled the sausages.

"Now the buns," Linda said. "Our buns are slightly larger than average, and perhaps a little doughy, but our customers like them like that."

"I like them like that," Milo said.

"The buns, too, are steamed. We put them in this basket inside the steamer." She opened a stainless steel door, and a puff of steam rose and added to the ruddiness of her face. "This board with the screen-door handles in a row is the bun bed. We put the bun to bed, like so." Linda placed the bun between two handles atop a piece of waxed paper. "Barely moist, and not wet—most important," she said.

"Absolutely," Milo said.

"Now, the fun begins," Linda said. "Into the bun, I insert the hot dog, and now, the green pickle relish along one side, and the chopped onion along the other." As she spoke, Linda applied the condiments. "Now, I grasp the mustard dispenser firmly, in the middle, and steadily just squeeze, while slowly moving it along the length of the hot dog."

"Marvelous," Milo said.

"Thank you. And now, we place the two tiny peppers,

right in the middle. Some customers can't handle this part."

"I can handle everything," Milo said.

"Two tomato wedges, and—this is what distinguishes a professional—the all-important celery salt goes on now"— Linda passed a saltshaker over the sandwich—"*before* we put the kosher half-sour pickle spear into the bun—along the side, see? We wrap, and there it is—a perfect hot dog." She handed it to Milo.

"It's beautiful," Milo said.

"Let's step in the back," Linda said. "Would you like to eat my hot dog?"

"Oh, yes," Milo said.

"Be my guest," Linda said. "While you enjoy it, I will tell you a few more things about the Rubinstein's Orthodox way of life. Then we'll come back here, and you, Milo, will create your first culinary masterpiece."

"I'm going to love it here," Milo said.

"I've got a feeling about you, Milo," Linda said. "You *are* going to love it here. I've seen them come, and I've seen them go, and unless I'm very much mistaken, like me you were born to work with wienies."

Phyllis MacGregor stood at one end of the meeting room made available by the Bandag Metaphysical Foundation, an organization made up of aging European pseudo-intellectuals, the purposes of which were conspicuously obscure. The membership of the B.M.F. had been dwindling steadily since it was founded in the late forties by disaffected Theosophists, Vegetarian-Spiritualists, and Christian Scientist hypochondriacs. The survivors made themselves useful by lending out their premises to groups, mainly self-helpers.

Phyllis was a small woman in an expensive-looking suit. As she spoke, she constantly ran her hands over her slender hips, her flat belly, her small, pointed breasts, and tiny buttocks. She also smiled—perfectly applied lipstick framed perfectly capped teeth. Her makeup was without flaw. She wore a tasteful amount of tasteful jewelry. She did not appear to be fifty-seven years old. She appeared to be brand-new.

"I was a failure," Phyllis told her audience. "I was a pathetic, weak, and utter failure. Some of you, I know, are looking at me and thinking, 'This woman is no failure. She is self-confident and poised. She is well groomed.' If you also knew that I was married to a wonderful man, and have a wonderful career in the field of travel consultancy, and have a wonderful son, a graduate of Brown University, who has written a novel, you might say, 'What failure? How a failure? I should be such a failure!'

"But it was not always like this. A few short years ago, it was all for nothing. For nothing was my fine husband—my third. For nothing was my fine position at Ahasuerus Travel Consultants. For nothing was my son, then about to enter Brown University. My life was destroyed! By this!"

Phyllis MacGregor ducked under the table behind which she stood, with such quickness that those who were witnessing her performance for the first time perceived her as having momentarily vanished into thin air. What she had actually done was squat and retrieve from a designer shopping bag a large amorphous object wrapped in plastic.

She reappeared. "Fat!" She slammed the object onto the table. It made a sound between thud and splat. "Twenty-five pounds of ghastly, ugly, life-destroying fat! You want to know what it looks like? This is what it looks like. And this is what kept me from being perfect, from enjoying my perfect life. This goddamned fat! It's what made me a failure." She was pummeling the package of fat, pounding it with her fist for emphasis.

The audience was riveted. Phyllis eyed the mass of fat with hatred and contempt that carried all the way to the back row, where Milton Cramer was sitting. Then she softened, she lifted her view to the fat people sitting on rows of creaky chairs, bought years before to seat renegade Theosophists, and barely adequate for heavy modern people. Her expression was one of love and compassion. "It made me a failure, and it's making you a failure. I don't have to tell you what every one of you knows in your deepest heart: If you're fat, you're despicable, worthless. It's a hard thing to hear, I know, but you all know it's true. And, I say it with love.

"It was as true of me as it is of you. Put this twenty-five pounds of blubber back on me, and I'd be less than nothing all over again. But that's not going to happen to me, because I am willing to . . . let's hear you say it . . ."

"Starve for success," the audience responded.

"That's right," Phyllis said. "I am never going back! Never! I live my life according to the four F rule. What is the four F rule?"

"Fight Fat, Fight Failure," the congregation chanted.

"The name of our program," Phyllis said. *"Fight Fat, Fight Failure.* For those of you who are with us for the first time, this program is possibly unlike others you have tried. We mince no words here. We confront reality, and we struggle against it. No one is going to coddle you here. Don't expect to be told that you're a good person inside, or that it's not your fault. Fat people are treated as an abomination by the rest of society—and why, Fat Fighters?"

"Because we *are* an abomination," the fat people shouted.

"And why do we say that?" Phyllis prompted.

"SHIT!" the Fat Fighters bellowed.

"And what does S-H-I-T stand for?"

"Self Hatred Is Truthfulness."

"That's right. If you didn't hate yourself, and rightly so, you wouldn't be here. I like to say that Fight Fat, Fight Failure is made up of people who didn't have character enough to kill themselves. And it's lucky we didn't because Fight Fat, Fight Failure shows us a better way out. What is that way?"

"Off yourself a pound at a time!" the fat failures shouted.

"That's right! If you hate yourself, despise yourself, loathe, reject, and detest yourself because you're fat—and who wouldn't?—just get rid of the fat part. Remember, fat is the worst thing there is. You can be a liar, a thief, a rapist, a murderer, a mass-murderer—being fat is worse.

"That's enough inspiration from me," Phyllis said. "Now it's time to hear from members of the group. Let's start with Larry. Larry, come up and talk to the people."

A pale, bald-headed man emerged from the audience and took Phyllis's place behind the table. "My name is Larry, and I was an appalling tub of rancid blubber," he said. There was enthusiastic applause. "I weighed two ninety-five at my most repulsive." Ooh's and aah's from the Fat Fighters.

"Now I weigh one forty-seven and a half, as of an hour ago," Larry said. (General applause.) "I try to weigh myself every two hours, and I recommend this to other Fat Fighters. It's quite simple to carry a small bathroom scale in a piece of hand luggage.

"It's a small price to pay for self-worth. And I have self-worth—self-esteem even. Not like it was. Not like the miserable, ugly, misshapen monster I used to be. A hundred forty-seven and a half pounds I weigh—and a hundred forty-seven and a half pounds I've lost. A whole person. And I'm not done yet. I intend to lose another twenty pounds—maybe twenty-five.

"Has it been easy? No, it has not. Every pound lost was torture. My health is affected because I lost so fast—just five months." (Wild applause.) "I lost my hair. I'm only thirty-two years old. I hardly have any strength, and I sweat all the time. There's something wrong with my gums, and there's blood in my urine. But, you know what? I feel great!" (Clapping.)

"I didn't drop one forty-seven and a half because of some health fad. I wasn't on some trivial fitness kick. I knew the diet I chose was dangerous—it was the hundred-percent meat-and-water one. But that wasn't of concern to me. I'll probably recover my health, though maybe not my hair." (Laughter.)

"No, Fat Fighters, I wasn't trying to become some kind of whole-grain nature boy. I just wanted to stop being an ugly, useless, worthless, squalid obscenity. I turned my self-hatred into creative aversion. And you can, too, you big fat tubs of excrement."

Larry resumed his seat amid an accolade. Phyllis spoke, "Now let's hear from Jennifer, who has been with us for only?"

"Two weeks," a tiny voice replied. Jennifer was an outsized young woman with straw-colored braids. Her blue jeans bulged everywhere, and she wore a sort of extra-large maternity blouse. "I hate myself," Jennifer said.

"You ought to, you big sow!" someone shouted.

"For years, I tried to compensate," she said. "I have a master's degree in history, and I'm an assistant principal in a high school."

"So what? You're a pig! A pile of shit! Disgusting!"

"I do volunteer work weekends."

"What do you volunteer as, a bus?"

"And I'm engaged to be married."

"Wonderful! What a deviant your fiancé must be, to want to climb up on a refuse heap like you!"

"And it all means nothing!" Jennifer was sobbing now.

"That's right, dear." It was Phyllis speaking now, her hand on Jennifer's beefy shoulder. "Your seemingly normal and successful life is just a façade to conceal your complete inadequacy and worthlessness. The only fact of your existence is that you are hideously obese, and undeserving of anyone's consideration, much less pity."

"Yes," Jennifer sniffed.

"But there's hope," Phyllis continued. "And what is that hope?"

"I might wise up before I explode?" Jennifer responded, barely audibly.

"Wise up before you explode!" Phyllis shouted.

The amplitude chanted, "Wise up before you explode!"

"Now go put your huge butt on a couple of chairs, Jennifer. You're doing fine, for a living garbage can."

8

Milton was becoming aware that the passage of time was an erroneous idea. When he was alive, he perceived it as having a sort of sequential organization. Now he knew that this was something he had been conditioned to accept. (Old Mr. Hirsch, the optician, had told him that, as an experiment, soldiers—or prisoners—had been fitted with eyeglasses with inverting prisms. After wearing them for a while, they adapted, mentally reinverting the images—and when they took the glasses off, everything appeared to be upside-down.) He had also known—he remembered, from a manuscript he had rejected, a science-fiction novel by Wiley Sinclair, an eccentric who regularly submitted texts, none of which ever were published—that in some thought systems, such as Hinduism, time was regarded as cyclical rather than linear, the same events taking place over and over. Now he was beginning to know that this was as inaccurate as the

Western notion of events beginning someplace, and heading toward an ultimate someplace else—the Creation, and much later, the Last Judgment, according to Christianity.

Time—that is to say, the way events were arranged—he now saw as a sort of maelstrom of tiny particles, lots and lots of them, in constant irregular motion, connecting and rearranging themselves kaleidoscopically. What led him to take this view was the fact that he could not only remember details of his life before death as they had appeared to him to take place when he was living—but he was also able to remember things which had not yet happened before he left the world in which they would happen. In other words, his life history continued, even though he was (as far as he knew) no longer a participant. Also, he was aware of long strings of causation arising from directions events had not taken—and these alternate histories seemed just as real as what he would have regarded as the one true account of his life, before his point of view changed so radically. Curiously, now that he knew so much more about what had happened, what was to have happened, what might have happened, what was still happening, and what was to happen than he could have possibly imagined—he scarcely cared at all.

Milton was sitting with the Four Tourists, so called because destiny had infinitely extended their respective holiday excursions. Most of the departed tended not to display much interest in their own former incarnations, much less those of others, but the mode of exit chosen for each of the Four Tourists offered amusement, having to do with their corpulence.

Lew, who had worked for twenty years without a vacation in the bowling equipment and supplies business in Chicago, sat down in a rented outrigger on the first day of his visit to Hawaii, and sank it. Three Kanakas dove down heroically to try to extricate him, but he was jammed in tight, and took the whole ride.

Tony had operated a small family restaurant in Detroit. He had Gone West while out West, on one of those mule-back rides, along precipitous cliff-face trails, down to the bottom of the Grand Canyon. The mules are famous for making their surefooted way along the outermost edge of the trail—trained to avoid scraping their burdens against the canyon walls, and thrilling their riders with a bird's-eye view of infinity. Tony got to the canyon floor long before anybody else, and at the same time as the mule.

Arthur, a native of Queens, New York, visited Coney Island, and broke a fifty-year safety record at the parachute jump in Steeplechase Park.

And Bob, a schoolteacher with a penchant for adventure, had gone up the Sepik River to a part of New Guinea where cannibalism was still said to be practiced. In fact, it had been abandoned a few years earlier, but the tribesmen he met made an exception in his case.

The Four Tourists, and Milton, sat in lawn chairs, their round bellies poking out from under their T-shirts, pudgy white knees protruding from their Bermuda shorts, and their fat feet, sockless, jammed into loafers. Each had a cigar.

"Supper in half an hour," Bob said.

"I smell potato pancakes," Lew said.

"I think you're right," Bob said.

"Usually, when they serve potato pancakes, they have pot roast," Tony said.

"That's OK by me," Arthur said. "I love pot roast."

"Who doesn't?" Bob asked.

"What was that shrimp thing at lunch?"

"I don't know. Never had it before. Good, though."

"I think that was Shrimp Chipotle."

"Chipotle?"

"It's Mexican."

"Sure was good."

"Mexican? You sure?"

"There are a lot of styles of Mexican cooking. It's not all enchiladas in red sauce."

"It was good."

"Do you guys ever talk about anything besides food?" Milton asked.

"Not often."

A long silence. The men savored their cigars.

"Casino's going to be good tonight," someone said.

"It isn't another comedy night, is it?" Milton asked. "No disrespect intended, but Almighty God uses the same material every time."

"It's not the material, it's the delivery."

"Ask me what's the most important thing for a comedian," Arthur said.

"What's the most important . . . ," Tony began.

"Timing!" Arthur shouted.

". . . thing for a . . ."

"Anyway, it's not a comedy night. Tonight it's Bardo."

"What's Bardo?" Milton asked.

"It's great. Come and see."

"It's not another of those audience-participation things, is it?" Milton had attended a couple of evenings of organized fun of that kind, and found them detestable.

"Bardo is Bardo," Arthur said. "In my opinion it's the second-best activity they have here."

"After sex," Milton said.

"After food," Arthur said. "Sex is third."

A distant third, Milton thought. He considered that he hadn't seen Natalie since his first day—and hadn't seen any other woman remotely of interest in that regard. More accurate, he hadn't seen any woman remotely interested in him.

"Some things never change," he said.

"That's true, of course," Lew said. "But there's a reasonable amount of variety, and what they serve is well-prepared, you'll have to agree."

"Absolutely," Bob said.

"I wasn't thinking about food," Milton said.

"Speaking of which . . . ," Tony said.

"Oh yes, the dining-room doors are open," Lew said.

"Well, let's put on the feedbag, shall we?"

Day's end at the Imago Luncheonette. Joe, the Korean proprietor, had handed Dr. Alan Plotkin a white paper bag containing a substantial amount of cash, and a cheese Danish, and was busy swabbing the floor. Plotkin donned an outsized topcoat, with chesterfield collar, and a derby hat. He paused at the door.

"See you tomorrow, Joe."

"Remember, you've got an eight A.M. Ms. Nussbaum," Joe said.

"Oh, yeh. The ophidiophobe. Better make it bacon instead of sausages with my breakfast omelette, Joe."

"Right. Have a good time tonight, Doc."

"Of course."

Parked outside was Plotkin's L7, in its day the biggest and most luxurious automobile BMW had ever made, black and dusty, the carpeted floorboards strewn with professional journals and old racing forms. He lowered himself into the commodious leather seat, disabled the alarm system, lit a Hoyo de Monterrey double corona, inserted a CD of Fritz Wunderlich singing Schubert lieder, brought the powerful engine to life, and pulled out into traffic.

Fifteen minutes later, having arrived in a scruffy neighborhood of small frame dwellings and brick warehouses, Plotkin entered the decommissioned and converted synagogue in which he lived, hurled his coat into a corner, sailed his derby into another, whipped off his tie, grabbed his set of bongos, and joined the perpetual, nonstop Mardi Gras, Walpurgisnacht, and hootenanny he had initiated twelve or thirteen years earlier. Fifty or sixty people were already going full tilt, making all the noise they could, dancing, singing, shouting, eating, drinking, necking, smoking marijuana, and affirming life.

By one in the morning, the individuals making up the band of celebrants had renewed themselves twice, and Plotkin in shirtsleeves was dancing with his arms above his head, accompanied on the flamenco guitar by Shep Nesterman, a local artiste who more or less lived in Plotkin's house.

When Plotkin finally lurched off to bed, he broke up a chess game in his sleeping chamber. The players were a resplendently attired little man and an irascible individual with a heavy accent. Like many of his guests, they were probable strangers to him—anyway, he could not remember having seen them before. The game was being kibbitzed by two heavy young women in a state of partial undress. Plotkin shooed the four out of his room, and they paused outside the open door, raised their glasses, and saluted him with a rendition of an anthem in some obscure language—it sounded Slavic. Plotkin could make out only one distinct word, something like "blint, blint, blint," repeated in the chorus—and as he fell asleep, it sounded sweetly in his ears.

The casino was packed when Milton entered. There was an atmosphere of excitement and good humor. The dear departed were seated along rows of tables, each with two cards, bearing the word BARDO printed across the top in block letters, with numbered squares in columns under each letter.

Charlie, wearing a straw boater and sleeve garters, was on stage, as usual. "And it's B, thirty-two! The number is B, thirty-two, boys and ghouls! B, thirty-two."

"Oh, no!" Milton muttered under his breath. A Bingo game! This was the big deal? This was *Bardo*? The Four Tourists were sitting together, stinking up the place with their lousy cigars, and waving baby dolls and rabbits' feet—lucky charms—over their Bardo cards. They were having a good time, that was obvious.

"It's R, eleven! R, eleven is the number! Who's going to *Bardo*? Who's going to win the mystery prize?"

Milton was about to make for the door, when someone grabbed his hand.

"Natalie!"

"Come sit with me. We can bring each other luck."

"You like this?" Milton asked, looking around at his fellow spirits hunched over their cards.

"I like the prizes," Natalie said.

Milton seated himself next to Natalie. There were already two fresh Bardo cards on the table before him.

"You know how to play?" Natalie asked.

"What's to know?" Milton asked. "That idiot Charlie calls out the numbers, and you put the little tiddlywinks on the appropriate squares."

"And you holler 'Bardo' if you get a line, vertical, horizontal, or diagonal," Natalie said. Could she be an idiot after all? Milton wondered.

"I was about to leave," Milton said. "What I wanted was to get a drink."

"But you can't get a drink," Natalie said. "We don't have alcohol."

"Yes. Why is that?" Milton asked.

"I think it's so the Muslims won't be offended," Natalie said.

"Muslims are *allowed* to drink in the afterlife," Milton said. "What's more, they get celestial maidens to pleasure them. I don't think there are any Muslims here. I think they've got their own place, and I want to go there."

"It's possible to have fun here," Natalie said, showing Milton her perfect teeth.

"O, five! It's O, five!" Charlie intoned from the stage.

"Oooh! I've got that one!" Natalie returned her attention to her Bardo cards.

Milton fiddled with his tiddlywinks. "This sucks *so* bad," he whined.

"Look! I've got another one!" Natalie said, plunking a wink on R, thirty-seven.

"They actually give prizes?" Milton asked.

"The best," Natalie said.

"Not a bottle of Black Label?"

"Better than that."

"Bardo! Bardo! I've got Bardo!" someone across the room shouted. It was Clara, a pleasant woman Milton had met once or twice in the reception area, outside the dining room.

"Let me just verify," Charlie said, moving over to Clara's table. "Yep, she's got it. You got Bardo, Clara."

Clara was waving her arms in the air, and squealing like a teenager.

"And you have won the mystery prize. Want to know what it is, Clara?"

"Is it oblivion? Is it oblivion?" Clara shouted excitedly.

"She wants oblivion?" Milton asked Natalie.

"Oblivion is a terrific prize," Natalie said.

"No, Clara," Charlie was saying. "It's not oblivion, but it's pret-ty good. It's . . . rebirth! Yes, Clara, you get a shot at doing it right. You are off to the staging area, where you will pick your new parents—then, it's down the old birth canal to a brand-new start."

"Lucky pup," Natalie said.

"That's lucky?" Milton asked.

"Oh, it's wonderful," Natalie said. "When you get reborn, you forget what you know now; start over as a baby."

"I wouldn't want that," Milton said, brushing the markers off his cards.

"You will," Natalie said. "You're just starting to know

everything. When you do, you'll wish you didn't. I hope she picks right."

"How do you pick right?" Milton asked.

"Well, as I understand it, when you're in the staging area, you wander around as a disembodied spirit. And you see all these pairs having intercourse—not just humans: animals and demons too. You get aroused. You want to have sex too—and finally you try to pry your way between a copulating couple. The instant you do that— zap! You're conceived. If you keep your wits about you, you can pick a couple of nice-looking humans—otherwise, you're going to be born as a cat or something."

Clara was surrounded by well-wishers. She was beaming with happiness.

"She wins another round, ladies and jerks," Charlie said. "Say goodbye, Clara. See you next time!"

Clara vanished into thin air.

"OK, folks, I'm mixing up the balls," Charlie said, swirling his hand in the oversized fishbowl that contained the numbered and lettered Ping-Pong balls. "Clear your cards, and get ready for a new game. It's a Big Prize this time. You thought Clara was lucky—well, someone might be even luckier. And here we go . . . it's D, thirteen! D, thirteen!"

Natalie was intent now, as was everybody else in the casino, except Milton. The pall of smoke from the Four Tourists' cigars hung over the tables, as Charlie called the numbers, and the chunky deadsters plunked their tiddly-winks.

"It's B, seventy! B, seventy!" Charlie called. "And no one has asked me what the Big Prize is."

"What's the Big Prize?" the inanimate obese shouted in unison.

"It's a doctor! And his wife's an attorney! In Lake

Forest, Illinois! No other children! A brand-new twelve-room colonial on three quarters of an acre. A Mercedes station wagon and a BMW! Vacations in Aspen and Key West! They're Episcopalians, gang. This is a good one!"

There were oohs and aahs from everyone, including Natalie.

"This is sickening," Milton said.

"Shh!" Natalie said.

"A, twelve, everybody! A, twelve!"

Milton had just noticed that Natalie was one square short of Bardo.

"R, fifty-four! R, fifty-four!"

"BARDO!" Natalie screamed. "BARDO! I've got it!"

"And so you have!" Charlie said. "Congratulations, Natalie! You're going to Mount Holyoke."

Natalie vanished.

"The next game is for a jackpot!" Charlie said. "We're playing for Natalie's room, now vacant. It's a single, friends, with a private bath and southern exposure."

Stunned as he was, Milton picked up a tiddlywink and prepared to listen to Charlie.

As soon as they had served their last customer, and handed over to the night shift, Milo and Linda hurried to Linda's apartment, which was not far from Rubinstein's Orthodox Hot Dogs.

While she drew a hot bath for Milo, Linda continued talking about her favorite subject. "All our products come from the Osterreicher Sausage Company of Green Bay, Wisconsin. They are an old family firm, very serious about sausage making. We use them because of their secret blend of spices. I have some here."

Linda sprinkled some powder from a large canister into the bath water. "Mr. Osterreicher—the third generation—always spends some time with me when he's in town; that's how I happen to have my own supply of the secret blend."

Milo smelled the same enticing aroma he'd noticed on first entering Rubinstein's.

"I'll just step out while you get comfortable in the bath," Linda said.

She left the bathroom, and Milo disrobed, folded his clothes on a chair, and lowered himself into the tub, which was very hot. No sooner had he done so, when Linda reappeared. She had nothing on but a big white apron, such as she wore at work, and was holding a large sponge.

"You lie back and relax. You've had a hard and, I might add, distinguished first day as a hot-dog man. Let Linda take care of you."

Milo had expected largesse when Linda had whispered in his ear, while he was preparing a takeout order of foot-longs, that she wanted him to come home with her, but he was unprepared for what turned out to be the bath of a lifetime. She scrubbed him, and frequently added hot water, until the bathroom was clouded with steam and the secret spice blend, her apron was soaking, and the two of them had reddened considerably.

Throughout the bath, and after, when they tumbled, dripping, into Linda's bedroom, the discussion of their profession continued, although what was said was increasingly punctuated by moans, gasps and cries.

"Protein-rich!"

"Bull meat! Bull meat and trimmings of sweet brisket!"

"Ah! Sweet brisket!"

"Hardwood! Hickory! Smoked!"

"Spices! Secret spices!"

"Oh! Knockwurst! Knockwurst!"

"I love them—natural *and* skinless!"

Linda's invention surpassed Milo's most frenzied fantasies. She actually kept a shaker of celery salt beside her bed, with which she augmented one of her many skills.

The grandest of grand finales had Milo going trans-
cendental all over, while Linda, articulate to the very
end, managed, "Milo . . . the . . . wiener . . . is . . .
good!"

And Milo saw that it was good.

12

"So?" Arnold Plotkin was seated at his usual table in the Imago Luncheonette, home of Psycho-Deli Associates.

"So, I went to see that editor—Milton Cramer," Milo said. "By the way, did he call you?"

"We already had a session. Thanks. Incidentally, the sandwich is on me . . . and have a napoleon too. They just came in fresh."

"Thanks, Doc. Anyway, I went to see him at his office, and we struck a deal," Milo Levi-Nathan said.

"He's going to publish your novel *Call Me Whale*?"

"No, it's not their sort of thing. But I am going to write a book for them."

"Do tell," said Plotkin, conveying a forkful of apple strudel to his mouth.

"It's what you advised," Milo said. "At first, I thought it would be prostitution to crank out a genre book for a flat fee . . . but, as you pointed out, it's experience, and I actually get to make some money by writing."

"Do they give you an outline, or what?"

"They have a writer's guide—it's about four pages— just gives some general rules. For example, in the case of science fiction (that's what they're having me write), no sexual intercourse between aliens and humans, if the aliens are darker than the humans."

"They must have a lot of sales in the South," Plotkin said.

"And there must be a sex act in the first thirty pages," Milo continued. "No anal sex, but you are encouraged to describe buttocks a lot. (I think that's just a personal preference of Cramer's.) Most of the rules are about sex. Oh yes, no cannibalism, but different species can eat each other."

"So, within certain limits, you get to write your own book?"

"That's right. I have to submit a detailed synopsis and get it approved, and then I'm off . . . and at the end of the road is a check for one thousand dollars."

"That's all? What if it becomes a best-seller? You'll never see another dime?"

"Then, I suppose I kill Cramer . . . and you too, ha ha."

"Still a little scared to express hostility without tacking on a little disclaimer . . . that 'ha ha,' at the end?"

"You're asserting your dominance as the psychotherapist. (Probably what motivated you to become one in the first place.) Because I threatened you."

"Very good! If being a writer doesn't work out, you might consider becoming a therapist. You could work as a lay shrink right here in the deli."

"Sometimes I wonder what it was you failed at before

going into head-shrinkery. (Just demonstrating that I can express hostility.) Anyway speaking of lay—I have more to tell you."

"Aha! Now we see why so frisky," Plotkin said.

"Get ready . . . Felix threw me out."

"Your stepfather fired you?"

"Yes! I have to admit, I was actually a little insecure about it at the actual moment . . . as though it hadn't been my dearest dream. He not only gave me the sack, he got me a job at Rubinstein's Orthodox Hot Dogs."

"I heard something about that," Plotkin said. "You're a counterman?"

"I'm a hot-dog man. It's the finest thing a man can be."

"Well, it's vitally important, I'll give you that. You like the job?"

"Love it," Milo said. "Simply love it. There's free nosh, and other side benefits."

"Such as what?"

"I made friends with a nice girl. Linda."

"And what's Linda like?"

"She's passionate about her work."

"And?"

"She gives great bath."

"Sometimes, I think that while I sit here tending to the ills of the mind, life is passing me by. She an attractive girl?"

"Going on two hundred pounds." Milo grinned.

"You dog, you."

"Yep, Doc. I'm free of the old maniac and his filthy parrots. I'm about to start writing for publication. I've got an important job. I eat for free. I've received the supreme gift—gratuitous sex, with the prospect of more. All of a sudden, I'm living in the sunshine."

"I'd say."

"So, I was figuring—let's cut the sessions down to one a week, what do you say?"

"It never fails," Plotkin said, running his finger around his plate, picking up strudel crumbs. "They get a little better, and then they turn on you."

Milton sat cross-legged on the carpet and gazed up at the tank. Swordtails, mollies, bettas, tetras, and angelfish glided to and fro under the brilliant aquarium light. On the floor of the tank, among the colorful pebbles, and glass marbles, a miniature deep-sea diver, with real bubbles rising from his helmet, stood beside a tiny treasure chest. The surface of the water, seen from below, was a rippling liquefied mirror, penetrated by a thermometer in a glass tube, reading 77°, and in reflection, ⊥⊥o.

The fish tank provided a focus by means of which Milton could obliterate the cranky whining of children, the utterances of mothers, the canned waiting-room music, and the peculiar doctor's-office smell. If he had been one of the fish, the glass walls of the tank would reflect inward, mirror-like, and he would see nothing but that peaceful, bright, rectangular world. He would hear nothing but the friendly sounds of bubbles and the electric pump. He would float weightlessly in the 77-degree water. It was almost like that. He had become expert at entering into the tank with his whole being.

His own mother, Martha, sat nearby, reading a magazine. When the nurse called his name, he would refuse to hear it, his trance would deepen, and Mrs. Cramer would have to shake him and half-lift him to his feet. Then, he would be pushed, shuffling, into the white corridor, and the examination room.

Stripped to his underpants, Milton sat on the examination table in the cold white room. The nurse had already pricked his finger, and shoved a thermometer far enough under his tongue to hurt him. He was whimpering, and his mother was making ineffectual soothing noises.

Dr. Klisterman, the pediatrician, entered, smelling of rubbing alcohol. Milton flinched.

"Ah! It's little fat stuff!" the doctor exclaimed. "Let's have a look at you."

Next came the ice-cold stethoscope, the hard wooden tongue-depressor, the rubber hammer, the hard *and* cold ear and nose speculum, and the thumping, poking, and instructions to breathe, not to breathe, to say "Ahh!" and "Ninety-nine."

"Well, he's just a little butterball," Klisterman said. "Looks like a little female, sitting there, with the fat belly, and the little breasts. Go outside, tubby, and tell the nurse I said to put you on the scale."

This was ritual. Milton would go out into the hallway in his underpants, and the nurse would conduct him to a scale. He would stand on the scale in his bare feet, while a steel rod was brought into contact with the top of his head—to measure his height. This time, when he opened the door of the examination room, another boy, also in his underpants, about Milton's age, and slightly less fat, was waiting for him. The opening of the door was the boy's cue.

"Fatty, fatty! I lost five pounds, why can't you?" the boy chanted automatically, and ran into another examination room. Milton turned and saw his mother and the doctor, nodding and smiling.

"What a good idea, Doctor," Mrs. Cramer said.

"An object lesson for your little tub of lard, and reinforcement for the other boy," Dr. Klisterman said. "A pediatrician has to be a psychologist."

"You certainly understand them."

"I'm always learning," the doctor said.

After the examination, in the doctor's private office, with the big desk and the leather chairs, Milton and his mother sat opposite the healer of children.

"Nothing wrong with him, Mrs. Cramer—but, as I've told you before, we have to do something about his obesity." To Milton he said, "Obesity. That means you're fat, young man. It's very unhealthy to be fat—and no one will like you. You understand?"

Milton whimpered.

"I suggest you take that blubber off your son before he turns into a circus freak. Here's a diet." Dr. Klisterman handed Mrs. Cramer the diet, a few sheets printed across the top with the name of a manufacturer of pharmaceuticals and suggested menus for breakfast, lunch, and dinner printed below. Neither Dr. Klisterman nor Milton's mother appeared to remember that they'd had this identical exchange more than once before. Milton remembered, but said nothing.

"Feed him this and nothing else. See me in three weeks. The girl will give you an appointment."

Mrs. Cramer folded the diet sheets and put them into

her purse. Milton was steps and seconds away from being free of Dr. Klisterman and the office. Klisterman had given him a lollipop—the doctor's-office kind, with the semiflexible twisted paper loop instead of a rigid stick, which might cause injury—root beer flavor, Milton's favorite.

Then the downward elevator ride—in every way more satisfying then the upward one—and outside into the streets of downtown. Next stop would be lunch in a restaurant, where Milton would be allowed to order anything he wanted, and a hot butterscotch sundae for dessert. His mother would smile indulgently across the table, and he would talk with her, and have her all to himself. She was apologetic and guilty for the discomfort he had suffered at the doctor's, and, in advance, for the diet of grapefruit halves, dry toast, skinned chicken by the ounce, and portions of spinach and kale, which she had solemnly resolved to prepare for him, and supervise diligently—starting the very next morning.

After lunch they would visit the book department in the gigantic downtown Woolworth's, where again he'd be allowed to choose whatever he wanted. Curious books they had at Woolworth's—such as Milton never saw in the branch library—stubby, thick novels printed on cheap paper that tore easily. The books weighed hardly anything, for all their bulk, and had stories about Popeye and the Shadow, and Secret Agent X-9.

Woolworth's also had a baked-goods counter, and Mrs. Cramer would buy a chocolate-strawberry layer cake, Milton's favorite, to serve at home after supper, as a sort of farewell to good things for Milton.

After never more than a day and a half, Milton, and his mother, would forget all about the diet.

14

Sunday lunch at the MacGregors': The table is piled high with bologna—sliced fresh from the deli counter—American cheese, pickle relish, mayonnaise, mustard, an extra-large loaf of enriched white bread, family-size bottles of root beer and ginger ale, two giant bags of potato chips—barbecue and sour cream-and-onion flavors—and a platter of Ring Dings, Ding Dongs, Devil Dogs, and Twinkies.

The family group includes Phyllis Levi-Nathan Mac-Gregor, her son, Milo, and Milo's stepfather, Felix. The conversation is sporadic. The slapping of bologna on white bread, slathering of mayonnaise, pouring of soda, smacking of lips, and guzzling, munching, muffled growling, and belching is continuous.

"Lookit him. Lookit your son. A slob. An elephant!" Felix muttered, pointing at Milo with his little finger while dislodging a food fragment from his bridgework with the nail of his thumb.

"Milo is just fine, Felix," Phyllis responded. "You're jealous of him, because he reminds you of my first husband."

"I never met your first husband. He vent like a bullet vhen he laid eyes on dis monster. He left it to me to feed and clothe deh miserable bestid."

"Milo was almost a grown man before I ever met you," Phyllis said. "You never fed him or clothed him."

Milo complacently shoveled in the food during this exchange. He was used to it. It went on all the time.

"Denks God, I didn't hev to feed him and clothe him," Felix said. "It vould break Rothschild to feed an ox like dis. But I gave him employment. For dis alone, I should have deh Nobel Prize."

"Employment? You gave him involuntary servitude," his wife rejoined. "You wouldn't know anything about it, but we had a war in this country to end slavery."

"Avraham Lincoln freed deh schvartzehs? I know all about it. And he vasn't no slave. From a slave I vould have gotten some vork outta him."

"So how are you, Mom?" Milo asked. "How are things at work?"

"Things are slow at Ahasuerus Travel Consultants," Phyllis said. "But I'm doing very well with the fat people. I have two groups of thirty, twice a week. As a group leader, I get fifty percent of the fees. My only expense is twenty dollars for the room—so it's six hundred forty dollars clear for four hours' work. You can't beat that."

"Do you think you're helping them?" Milo asked.

"They're unhappy people, son," Phyllis said.

"Elephants!" Felix interjected.

"Mom? You don't think I'm unhappy, do you?" Milo asked.

"I hope not," Phyllis responded. "I hope you have better things to do with your evenings than sit around having abuse heaped on you for twelve dollars."

"I prefer to come here and get abused for free," Milo said.

"Ha! I know what he's doing evenings!" Felix chortled. "Rubinstein told me all about it. He's schtupping a Polish girl from vork—a slut!"

"Linda may be a slut, but she's a fine person," Milo said. "And Rubinstein is a better boss than you ever were."

"Rubinstein is crazy," Felix said. "He has a place vit food, and he lets you in dere? He'll go bankrupt inside a year. You'll nosh him into chepter eleven, you kangaroo!"

"I'm writing a book," Milo said, ignoring his stepfather.

"Another one?" Phyllis exclaimed. "Such a good boy!"

15

BOOK PROPOSAL
MAMZERS FROM CASSIOPEA
by
Milo LaFontaine [Levi-Nathan]
Chapter One

The year is 1948. The scene is the home of Albert
Einstein, in Princeton, New Jersey. Einstein is
conversing with a friend, Heinrich Blucher,
another German intellectual refugee. They make
small talk:

"Ach, Albert, I notice zat you neffer vear
socks. Vhy is zat?"

"I haf observed zat it takes approximately
seventeen seconds, on zuh average, to put on
socks. Zis amounts to two minutes per veek,
which adds up to nearly hundred und zhirty-nine

hours in a lifetime of eighty years--or about fife und zhree quarter days."

"Und you do not put on zuh socks in order to save all zis time?"

"No--I do not put on zuh socks because zuh elastic makes zuh little red marks aroundt mine ankle--but zuh calculations are amusing, nicht wahr?"

"Ja, Albert. Now, let me see if I get zis right, zuh M is mass, ja? Und zuh C is zuh shpeed of light. Und mass und zuh shpeed of light multiplied by itzelf equals zuh big energy, ja?"

"Alvays zuh questions about zhis, Heinrich. I like better vhen you talk about zuh abstract expressionism."

. . . and so on. Gradually it emerges that Blucher has come to see Einstein because he has learned about a rash of UFO sightings, and a government coverup. There have been a number of mass abductions, in which populations of whole towns have disappeared--except fat individuals, who remain behind, somewhat confused but unabducted, and relatively unharmed.

"I have zhought und zhought about zis, Albert. Und I haf come to no conclusion. Mine mind is in a fuck."

"A fuck?"

"Ja, a fuck."

"Your mind is in a fuck?"

"Ja, ein complete fuck."

"A fuck, you say?"

"Ja."

"Vhat has a fuck got to do vith it?"

"It is like a fuck. In mine mind. A mind fuck. You know vhat is it a fuck?"

"I zhought I knew."

"A fuck! A fuck! You know: 'Zuh fuck comes in on little Katz's feet?' "

"Ah, a fuck!"

"I said, a fuck."

Einstein ponders, "Hmm, Heinrich. Zis is most interesting. I haf often vondered vhy some people are fat. What has caused zis genetic propensity to put on zuh schmaltz? Perhaps zuh fat individuals are in some vay protected from zis extraterrestrial zhreat."

"Ach! Sehr interessant, Albert. Zo you zhink zat in some vay zuh fatsos are immune to zhese ozhervorldly depredations?"

"It vould stand to reason, Heinrich. Gott does not play dice vit zuh universe."

16

Las Vegas night in the casino. Charlie is wearing his croupier's visor. The overweight obsolete crowd around the table.

"Get your bets down, ladies and gargoyles. And he rolls! And it's Little Joe from Baltimo'! The point is four! He rolls . . . and it's seven-out! Next shooter!

"And it's . . . oh my! What an honor. Ladies and grease-balls, it's the Highest Roller, the Holy Roller, the Pre-eminent Player, the Omniscient Odds Maker, the Blessed Bone Thrower, the Undisputed Champion of Abyssinian polo, Congo croquet, and Memphis marbles, the Great Gamester Himself. He flutters, we shudder. He shakes the bones, we quake and moan. He rattles the ivories, we go for our rosaries. He plays, we pray. He wins, we sin. Get ready, get ready! He's going to toss the cubicon.

"Ladies and gluttons, fade Him, fade Him, all fade Him! Shoot the works! Almighty God, in Person, is going to motivate the galloping dominoes!"

17

Dear Milo—

I am herewith returning your sample of *Mamzers from Cassiopea*, which certainly confirms your ability as a writer.

However, it doesn't seem to be *precisely* what we're looking for here at Harlon House. First, setting a Sci-Fi story in 1948 would possibly turn off a lot of readers. Then, tho I haven't checked it, including Einstein as a character might give rise to permissions problems if there's an estate, or if the character has been optioned by media.

Couldn't you create a modern scientist, completely fictional, and perhaps a little less funky than A.E.? I don't know Blucher—is he a real person also? (See 'graph above.)

I'd like to see a little more contrast here, possibly a woman assistant, which would give you the option of a romantic sub-theme. Maybe they could have a sort of tongue-in-cheek flirtatious relationship? A useful device I often suggest to writers, is to picture your favorite movie stars as the characters—adds realism.

I'd lose the German accents, and the F-word. I, for one, couldn't see the point of that exchange—and who's Katz?

Next, abduction by UFO. Not out of the question, but there has been a lot published on that theme.

Fat people are out. Sorry. You and I are both chubbies, so you know this is house policy, and nothing to do with me. Another thing we never do is include hard science, so they shouldn't discuss Math. Sad commentary, but our readers won't get it. Stick to the "dilithium crystals" and "warp fractals" sort of thing—and keep the explanations short!

Here's a tip I hope you'll take to heart. Start with action. That's what grabs the reader. Pacing is everything.

Love "God does not play dice with the universe!" That original?

Strong writing! Don't get discouraged. Be well, do good work, and keep in touch.

Best,
Milton

18

When the meeting of Fight Fat, Fight Failure broke up (the Fat Fighters, in unison, had given a loud roar, and charged out of the meeting room with their hands over their heads, like a football team taking the field), Milton lingered behind. He had been slightly worried about whether there would be, and how he would deal with, a period of informal socializing after the proceedings ended—the Fat Fighters seemed so aggressive, not to say fierce. As it turned out, they thundered down the stairs and burst out into the street—gone in no more than a minute.

Phyllis MacGregor hefted her crocodile attaché, containing $700 in cash, firmly gripped a can of Mace, held at the ready in her free hand, and was gone in the next minute, pausing only to hand twenty dollars through the open half of a Dutch door in the hallway to Laszlo Gegenschein, the resident caretaker. Milton was alone with the folding chairs.

Almost alone. Becoming aware of another presence, he turned, and saw the woman who had testified last, standing like one waiting for a bus, with a huge soft leather shoulder bag, and clutching a cape or serape woven of wool in some Third World country.

"It's Jennifer, isn't it?" Milton asked.

"Yes. I'm too self-conscious to yell and run out like the others."

"They do that every time?"

"Yes. I'm also too depressed."

Jennifer moved closer to Milton. He noticed that she had a pretty face and a tendency to smile. Her eyes were brown and conveyed intelligence, and none of the melancholy which appeared to characterize everything she said.

"This was my first time," Milton said.

"I've been coming for two weeks," Jennifer said. "Twice a week. This was my fifth meeting. I'm not getting it."

"You don't think it's helping you?"

"No. It doesn't help at all. I've tried everything else."

"But you stood up and talked," Milton said. "I'm sure I couldn't do that. I thought what you said was very moving, and took a lot of courage." Milton noticed that she had handsome hands and smelled of sandalwood soap.

"It didn't take any courage," Jennifer said.

"They said all those horrible things to you."

"I hear that stuff on the street every day. People think it's perfectly all right to talk to a fat woman like that."

"Awful."

"The problem here is that I can't develop any creative self-loathing. The abuse just isn't working."

"You said you hated yourself," Milton put in. He wondered what it would be like to touch her hair, and was surprised at how much the thought excited him.

"I lied. I have a tendency to say what I think people want to hear. I lied about my education and my job too, and I have no financé."

"Somehow that news fails to disquiet me," Milton said.

"José Ferrer in Cyrano," Jennifer said. "I'd judge you to be a late-movie buff rather than a Lit major."

"Both actually," Milton said, delighted that someone had finally picked up on a gambit he'd employed for years with no response.

"So what's your name, anyway?" Jennifer asked, poking Milton playfully with a forefinger.

"It's Milton."

"Pleased to meet you, Milton," Jennifer said. She smiled for real now, gorgeously.

"Have you eaten?"

"Frequently," Jennifer said. "And I'm about to do so again, right? You *are* inviting me?"

"Oh, yes," Milton said. "Are you . . . I mean . . . on a . . . diet . . . or anything?"

Jennifer elbowed Milton in the paunch and giggled impishly. "Let's say I tend to be up for anything."

"Chinese all right?"

"You know a good place?"

"I think you'll be . . . amused." Milton offered his arm, Jennifer took it, and they moved toward the door.

"Dammit! That's just what I mean!" Jennifer hissed.

"What?"

"See this? We talk for three minutes, you invite me to supper, and all of a sudden I'm in a good mood. I can't

stay depressed, or despise myself worth diddly-do-dah."
She smiled up at Milton. He liked that she came up just to
his shoulder.

"Still," Milton said, "you gotta eat."

"Do I ever," Jennifer said.

On Wednesday afternoons in fine weather, Alan Plotkin drove out into the country, sometimes alone, sometimes with two or three colleagues. His destination was a rural airfield from which the *Eros und Thanatos* Skydivers, a sporting club made up of psychotherapists, made its weekly ascent. The ride was always festive and boisterous, with a stop enroute at Luigi's Lean-to, a roadside stand purveying outstanding grilled Italian sausage sandwiches, heaped with onions and peppers and dripping grease. Fortified with two or three doubles, served on magnificent grinder rolls available nowhere else, and many frosty bottles of beer, the ebullient alienists would convene with their fellows at the Eugen Bleuler Memorial Clubhouse, a corrugated metal shed next to the hangar, and suit up for their jump.

Plotkin's own jumpsuit had been supplied by the King Size Company, of Hingham, Massachusetts, and was a mighty conflagration of orange, red, and yellow. His chute was also special-ordered, extra-large, and emblazoned with a crimson lightning bolt.

A trusty old DC-3, with cargo door and seats removed, would be warming up on the apron, and the happy headshrinkers would pile on, joking and shouting. Once aloft, protocol would be enforced by the jumpmistress, Meesha, a willowy school psychologist, who would have commanded everyone's attention, even without the black skintight costume with cutouts, and the very special boots. Meesha did everything by the book, and tolerated no high jinks once at proper altitude and above the jump zone. She would instruct the airborne analysts to stand up, hook on, stand in the door, and tumble out in strict accordance with usage and tradition. The only variation in routine was that the hurtling healers would shout, "Kakorhaphiophobia!" rather than "Geronimo!" as they cleared the plane.

These weekly jumps had gone on for years, and every August, the club would descend en masse onto the beach at Martha's Vineyard, with devices emitting colored smoke taped to the heels of their boots.

Plotkin projected himself into the slipstream, felt the wind rushing in his ears, heard the roar of the engines, and felt the snap as the static line pulled the canopy out of the pack—then the satisfying tug and bounce, and the snugging of his harness as the parachute deployed and created the sensation of reversing his fall and causing him to rise.

He swiveled his head, checked the suspension lines, and adjusted his position. The plane was high above him, and moving away now, the sound of the engines fading. He had located the white circle marking the jump zone, and manipulated the shrouds. He was moving right for it in the still air. Now he could take some time to enjoy the beauty of the landscape, and the silence. This was what he came back for—the silence mainly—and exquisite lightness. Like a colossal snowflake, he wafted, his mind clear, his senses amplified, euphoric, blissful—at one with nature, and close to God. He unzipped a pocket of his jumpsuit, removed a Snickers bar, unwrapped it, and was able to finish the last leisurely bite before he had to busy himself with negotiating his landing.

Laszlo Gegenschein watched Milton and Jennifer scamper down the stairs.

"Ah, young people," the old caretaker said to himself. "Full of life and energy. The boy appears to be destined to die soon. Such a nice, fat young man. It's God's will, of course, so nothing to worry about."

Gegenschein folded chairs and carried them four at a time to one end of the room, where he placed them leaning against the wall in neat stacks of four—seven stacks, and two chairs left over, all at precisely the same angle, and with uniform spaces between the stacks. He stood and looked at his work.

"OK, chairs? You're satisfied?"

One stack of chairs did not appear completely identical to the others, and he went forward and adjusted it minutely.

"Now, better. On these chairs have sat some of the finest minds of the twentieth century. Seekers, spiritual persons, artists, philosophers have used these chairs. Madame Blavatsky, Gurdjieff, Ramakrishna, Mary Baker Eddy, Bob Dylan, C. J. Jung, Kirpal Singh, Nina Kiriki Hoffman, Ho Chi Minh, Rolzup, David Isay, the Mad Guru, Jackson Pollock, Conan Doyle, Laird Cregar, Krazy Kat, Trotsky, Bill Moyers, they all came here at one time or another."

Now the old man got a push broom, and meticulously swept. As he swept, mantras, chants, aphorisms, homilies, sayings, dicta, maxims, precepts, illustrations, and instances bubbled up in his mind as from a fountain, and were spoken half-aloud. He was remembering fragments of the decades of lectures, talks, discussions, workshops, debates, therapies, panels, meetings, self-help groups, meditations, services, recitals, performances, and readings that had taken place in these very premises—situated on the top floor of the old two-story building, which was shared by a tiny Orthodox Jewish congregation, a rehearsal studio, and a hat-blocking and -cleaning establishment.

Having swept the room as no room is ever swept, Laszlo Gegenschein paused in the doorway, his hand on the light switch, and had another look. He was checking whether everything was perfect, and remembering.

"So many bullshitters," the old man said, clicked the switch, and locked the door.

He went to his cubicle in the hall, a combination utility closet, concierge's room, and his bedroom for the past six years. There he placed for safekeeping a manila envelope someone had left behind, got his hat and coat, locked the Dutch door, went down the broad staircase and out into the street, where he set out in the direction of Gypsy Bill's Hungarian-American Cafeteria and Bakery.

"Such a nice, fat young man," Gegenschein said to the empty street and the night air.

21

The words "beech" and "book" derive from the Anglo-Saxon word *boc, bece,* or *beoce.* Ancient runic tablets are believed to have been formed of thin boards of beech-wood; hence, a book was something written on beech. (The origin of this word is thought to be identical to the Gothic *boko,* letter, and *bokos,* writing.)

The European beech *(Fagus sylvatica)* often grows to a height of one hundred feet or more. It has dark-gray bark and shining leaves which remain on the tree most of the winter. The European species is used in the United States as an ornamental tree. One of the most beautiful varieties is the copper beech, with red leaves. Purple beech, with bronze-purple leaves, and the cut-leaf beech are also ornamental varieties of the European tree. There is a weeping, or pendulous-branched variety.

The root system, and sometimes lower branches which make contact with the ground, may evolve new individuals. Thus, old trees may be surrounded by a thicket of younger trees produced in these ways rather than from seed. Often the progenitor has ceased to exist, and a hollow circle of beeches results.

Older beech trees often develop a unique, not to say curious and grotesque, aspect, especially in winter. The thick trunks acquire bulbous and irregular contours, suggestive of deformed torsos, and the limbs have been likened to withered and wasted arms of the very old. The roots above ground suggest bunioned and arthritic feet, and many an illustrator of fairy tales has exploited this sinister quality in depicting an eerie scene, with beech trees menacing or snatching at Hansel and Gretel, or other unfortunates at the mercy of a malevolent supernatural forest.

In the park near the apartment building in which he lived, Milo Levi-Nathan discovered a fairy circle of weeping beeches. The original tree, a son of a beech from Eastern Europe, had long since been cut down by the Parks Department.

Milo liked to stand in the canopied, dome-like space, concealed from passersby by the pendulous branches, which reached almost to the ground. The trunks were carved with initials, dates, and commemorations of real, or wished-for, couplings and orgies which might have taken place in the secluded spot. He felt a certain vegetable energy when he stood there, and a connection with something extremely distant and vague. He felt he ought to write about the beech grove, but he had so far been unable to determine how to go about it.

Bela Kramarchykowicz, Milton's paternal grandfather, was a son of a bitch from Eastern Europe. He came from the village of Blint, which was thought to be somewhere southwest of Uzhgorod, and was or had been part of Russia, Romania, Czechoslovakia, or Hungary—or all of them. Nobody remembered, and possibly nobody knew, or cared, even back there and back then.

Bela was a self-possessed and taciturn individual, and not given to sentimental reminiscence about life in the old country. He was no storyteller. For the most part, he found expression in delivering himself of frightening curses and threats, nor was he inhibited about applying an enormous fist to the side of one's head by way of emphasizing a point. So Ignatz, his son, and certainly Milton, knew little enough about their roots, except the surmised idea that things must have been rough in Blint.

Rough wasn't the half of it. The residents of Blint

would have regarded serfdom as a big step up the social
ladder. They would have jumped at the chance to be
slaves, had anybody been willing to make them the offer.
Which nobody would have been, given that Blintites
appear to have been uniformly aggressive and unpleasant
to a stunning degree. In fact, stunning was a daily occur-
rence, as the villagers were more than quick to pursue one
another with massive *chalyatchkie* sticks, and apply them
energetically.

Aside from trying to brain their neighbors with beech
boughs, these remarkable people, who had been skipped,
not only by modern times, but the Reformation, the
Renaissance, the good bits of the Middle Ages, and in fact
almost all of cultural history, spent their time gathering
"mast," the fruit of the *Fagus sylvatica*, known everywhere else as provender for swine, or as a substitute, in
times of famine, for kasha or buckwheat groats, already
not a dish of choice for those who have a choice. In Blint
it was practically all they ate.

About the only feature of Blint that bears mentioning is
the long history of para-, and super-, in addition to sub-,
normal manifestations. Vampires and werewolves were,
and had always been, as common as municipal scandals in
other places. Mysterious lights in the woods, weird crones
with the power to curse and heal, citizens who had
acquired bizarre physical and mental anomalies after
encountering strange beings on moonlit forest paths
(giants, dwarfs, uncategorizable monstrosities, and the
very popular man with three lights in his belly), would
have been noted regularly in the daily newspaper, if they
had had a daily newspaper, and if any of them had been
able to read one.

Andar Kramarchykowicz, Bela's father, was the most

objectionable man in Blint, and the one most likely to encounter something spooky on a dark night. It was something Andar had started, and which Bela had finished, or nearly finished, which necessitated Bela's abrupt departure to as far away from Blint as he could get, which turned out to be America.

When she was a little girl, playing with her sister and their friends, Jennifer Gusdorf used the terms "pig," and "fat pig," and "big fat pig" as pejoratives like the other children. It was some time before it began to dawn on her that she really was one. She was a big fat pig only to other children. The adults referred to her as a "little pig."

She could remember the first time the use of the term had registered. There had been some confusion at an outing of the Gusdorf clan. Her parents had someplace else to go, and deposited her at the picnic grounds in the park, in care of her Aunt Susan. Then they had gone away, possibly to come back later, or maybe Aunt Susan and her family would take Jennifer home at the end of the day. Whatever arrangements had been made, they had not been explained to Jennifer, or she had not understood them. Apparently, provision for Jennifer to eat had been overlooked—each family being responsible for its own lunch. Jennifer's nuclear unit was not there, so she assumed she'd been attached to the cousins' contingent— Aunt Susan's kids.

Jennifer played with her cousins, swam in the lake, participated, ineptly, in some organized games, and then, with the other kids, approached the wooden table-and-bench affair, where fried chicken, potato salad, and other traditional picnickery were being consumed by the adults. The cousins jammed themselves in along the bench, and set to. There wasn't space for Jennifer, so she stood by, expecting one of the adults to fix her a plate, or make a space for her, or somehow take care of her. She hadn't actually figured out the options—she was eight years old, and used to having awkward social situations put right by grownups. Nobody paid her the least attention. The Lipizzan family, Aunt Susan's family, were whipping into their lunch, without giving her a glance. She might have said something, but she didn't know what to say. Bursting into tears would have been a possibility had she been much younger, but as it was, all she could do was stand, confused, and edge a little closer.

It seemed to Jennifer that a lot of time passed. The picnic was pretty much consumed, when Uncle Fred finally noticed her. In front of Uncle Fred was an open package of sesame cookies, mostly intact. It was the only food on the table that had not been reduced to shreds. By this time, Jennifer was impossibly hungry.

"Want some?" Uncle Fred asked her, holding the package by one corner, and causing it to pivot across the table in Jennifer's direction. A miserable meal, the one item left over by the ravenous kids and adults, presumably because the cookies were as tasteless and dry as they looked—but Jennifer took a step forward and began to raise a hand to table level.

"I'll bet you do," Uncle Fred said, pivoting the cookies back, toward himself and away from Jennifer. "You little pig."

It made a big impression on her. Later, even into adulthood, she would reason that the Lipizzans had mistakenly thought she had eaten with her parents and siblings, and in their simple way, assumed the obvious, that she was making the rounds of other tables in the picnic grove, begging for scraps like a dog. This was how she comforted herself, and rationalized not hating her relatives and wishing them dead and in Hell.

In school, after she had gotten out of the primary grades, and the "big fat pig" period, it was not so much a matter of what she was called, but that she was not called. Jennifer was not called by name, because most of the children did not know her name. The teachers, of course, knew her name, or at least had written it down in their grade books—but she seldom heard it spoken. As much as girls were progressively called upon less in the classroom as they ascended grades in school, Jennifer was called on less yet, diminishing to almost not at all.

It may have been that some teachers refrained from calling on Jennifer to spare her the embarrassment of being exposed to the scrutiny, and cruel comments, of her fellow pupils. Or it may have been that they assumed she was stupid because of her inhibited way of moving and round impassive face, which was perceived as floating, avoiding eye contact at the back of the room, among the other idiots, misfits, and fatties.

She did A work, got B's (because she did not participate in class), and went on to high school and college, where she had identical experiences.

At home with her family, Jennifer was outspoken, cheerful, and funny. They loved her, and often said they did not think of her as fat. They did not think of her as cook, cleaner, laundress, shopper, and unpaid domestic either, but she did most of the work of the house, and was by far the last of her sisters to move away.

She'd had two love affairs, the first with a hippie handyman and drug dealer, for whom she carried bundles of roofing shingles, lumber, tools, and bales of marijuana across state lines in the trunk of her car. Much later, after the hippie had moved on, she met an aging desert rat while on vacation out West, and for two weeks each year assisted him in transporting petrified wood and ancient Indian artifacts, which he stole from national parks. Both men were involved with other women while with Jennifer, which she was expected to tolerate, and did.

Jennifer had experienced twenty-six diets, two summers at weight-reduction camp, two hospital-administered weight-loss programs, one total fast, five self-help groups, three courses of nonstandard medical treatment (one of which had landed her in the hospital), three courses of approved medical treatment (one of which had landed her in the hospital), hypnosis, a staple in her ear, membership in a meditating cult, six years of regular exercise at health clubs, and eight years of psychotherapy by the time she went to a Chinese restaurant with Milton Cramer.

BOOK PROPOSAL
VAMPIRES OF DENDROS
by
Milo Sabatini [Levi-Nathan]
Chapter One

The office of Nate Marlowe, scientific detective
and two-fisted hero. Nate is 300 pounds of ani-
mal cunning and advanced physics. He's a tough
guy with a tender heart, thought to be corrupt,
but really honest--lights his smokes with a
wooden kitchen match that he strikes on his
thumbnail.

Enter Barbara Goldberg, a knockout redhead,
and there's plenty of her. Nate gives her the
double-O. Barbara starts out leaning on Nate's
desk, giving him a closeup of the Grand Tetons,

and winds up hanging onto the desk's corners with her black lace panties around her ankles while Nate conducts a vigorous investigation from behind--all with hardly a word of dialogue, just some snappy first-person description.

Curled up in a leather armchair, purring like a kitten, Barbara smokes a black Sobranie cigarette, and tells Nate her story. It seems she is the daughter of Zoltan Goldberg, the Nobel Prize—winning scientist. Zoltan has, of late, shown a tendency to vanish without trace for extended periods. Sometimes, late at night, he receives a strange visitor under conditions of secrecy in the mansion where he keeps Barbara and her two equally gorgeous and sex-starved sisters virtual prisoners.

"So? Happy families are all alike," Nate quips, studying her creamy thighs. "What do you need me for, beside the obvious?"

"It's the trees," Barbara says, her full lips trembling with fear. "The beeches."

"What about them?" Nate asks, thinking about kissing her on the mouth, hard.

"They move around at night."

Another loony dame, Nate thinks, but quite the piece of ass.

"You mean as in, the wind blows in the branches?" he asks.

"I mean as in, mornings the trees are not in the same spot they were in the day before," Barbara says, her green eyes wide.

"I have a friend, a doctor," Nate says. "He talks to people."

"Look, Mr. Marlowe . . . ," Barbara begins.

"I think you can call me Nate, after the toboggan ride we just took."

"Nate, I'm not crazy. Look at these."

From a Hermès bag, Barbara produces a set of Polaroids. It's evident to Marlowe's practiced eye that they aren't fakes. They show a vast manicured lawn, with stately copper beeches, all photographed from the same point--and it's clear that the beeches have changed their position from one picture to the next.

Marlowe decides to search Barbara exhaustively, overlooking nothing, after which they drive out to Zoltan Goldberg's mansion to reconnoiter, take measurements, and check out the sisters.

After a scene with all three Goldberg girls in an enormous bathtub made from a Roman sarcophagus, Nate is introduced to Zoltan. He cleverly pressures Goldberg to deliver the emmis about the whole geschichte, and an amazing recounting ensues.

It seems that the beech trees on the Goldberg estate, and all beech trees, are not of earthly origin. They are, Goldberg explains, vegetable-based spacecraft, and breeding colonies for a variety of alien resembling, in their decades-long larval stage, wads of chewed-up Fleer's Dubble Bubble bubble gum. These aliens ultimately evolve into vaguely humanoid creatures, small, with glowing lights in their abdomens. When they reach full maturity, which takes about a century, they take sustenance by extracting lipids from mammals--and in particular, humans.

"My God!" Nate exclaims, atypically expressing excitement. "You're saying they're fat-vam-
pires?"

"I'm saying that, and more," Zoltan Goldberg
continues. "Until now, only a few individuals
have reached maturity, mostly in Europe and
years ago. But the main fleet has landed and has
been on earth for the requisite period of time.
The Dendrosians are about to reach full maturity
all at once, and in great numbers. Once their
digestive systems have fully formed, the hunger
reflex will activate, and I am very much afraid
they'll suck the schmaltz out of every man,
woman, and child on the planet."

On the bulletin board outside the dining room, a notice was posted that hula classes would begin that afternoon in the casino.

A phonograph played Hawaiian music, a long folding table, covered by a paper cloth, was set with pineapple slices and cookies, and Charlie, wearing a grass skirt, stood ready to give instruction.

Nobody but Angela Podgorny showed up, and the lessons were discontinued until further notice.

26

Dear Milo—

Vampires of Dendros (great title!) actually got as far as the weekly meeting of our editorial board. I just wanted to get them acquainted with your work, because I am more confident than ever that you are a writer we will want to publish.

Only prob' with this one, of course, is that you're mixing two genres—Detective and Sci fiction. My opinion, which was seconded by the board, is that you should go with one or the other. (I'm hoping you choose Sci-Fi, 'cause we don't do any sleuth books.)

Board also was uneasy about the fat shamus—and the girl seemed to maybe be on the heavy side ("there was a lot to her"). Gotta remind you that thin is in, especially when it comes to the fair sex. Speaking of which (sex, that is), I thought you handled the subject very sensitively.

Trees in space! Where do you get those ideas?

Great work. Don't weaken. Keep in touch.

Best,
Milton

27

Surrounded and concealed by a vast cloud of cosmic dust, a nearly unthought-of object makes its way through the great darkness. More than sixty meters long, its central part is roughly cylindrical, thick, with irregular swellings and whorls. Both ends of the mass ramify, divide, branch, fork, and bifurcate into a complicated and delicate tracery.

This is not an incredibly unlikely item of space debris, but an even more unlikely something, going somewhere. It is being directed by rational thought, or anyway thought, or anyway something like thought, or instinct, premonition, biological directive, or fate.

An organic, naturally evolved entity, the object is also a craft of sorts, and has on board a sort of pilot, a singular pink wad, which is a separate organic entity, residing in the heart of the great floating host.

It is not, in its present state, capable of discrete rational thought, but can direct the motion of the great vehicle toward an environment which will provide what the pink wad will ultimately require when the next phase of metamorphosis takes place: esters of glycerin with carboxylic acids, such as palmitic, lauric, and stearic, which have sixteen or eighteen carbon atoms.

According to the laws of symbiosis, that same environment should be one in which the fibrous space vehicle can satisfy its particular requirements. In this case, Captain Pinkwadder and that which only God can make are proceeding at vegetable speed toward a planet known and loved by one and all.

BOOK PROPOSAL
THE DISKOUNTIKON
by
Milo Nuñez Cabeza de Vaca [Levi-Nathan]

THE UNIVERSE

The action of this series of books takes place
in that portion of the time-space continuum in
which the usual conditions are suspended.
Nothing is impossible, and that which is possible is transitory and provisional. Interaction
between life-forms, and life of nominal
non—life-forms, simultaneous appearance of
beings and events ordinarily separated by mil-
lennia, and violations of the rules of natural
history and physics are commonplace.

THE PREMISE

The Great Discount Pharmacy is the largest discount pharmacy ever conceived. Centrally located in time and space, the Great Discount Pharmacy serves the needs of uncounted life-forms from every world and time.

The parking has accommodation for over 178,000,000 vehicles of every description. And there are generally 336,000,000 vehicles cruising for a space.

The average visit to the Great Discount Pharmacy lasts three to four lifetimes, the first of which is spent looking for a parking place, and the last looking for that place again after visiting, or attempting to visit, the Great Discount Pharmacy. Most visitors never see the Great Discount Pharmacy, having been distracted by one of the improvised satellite pharmacies, containing only one or two thousand departments.

The Great Discount Pharmacy is often taken for the Christian heaven. You can get prescriptions and personal-care products. You can buy vitamins, contraceptives for hard-to-fit species, there's a photo-processing department, of course, and a foods department where you can get short-dated sausage products and cheese.

In the parking lot, murder is common, as is accidental death arising from one life-form's failing to recognize other life-forms as such. Common victims are germ people and pebble people--and, of course, parking-space men are crushed to death in great numbers.

BACKSTORY/INTRODUCTION

Events which precede the story proper are recounted by Blind Grapefruit, a street singer and Greek chorus.

Irvinge, a youth of pure heart and only son of Ratner, an itinerant funeral-director, from whom he has been separated, has grown to manhood alone in the vast interior of the Gogomobil, an obsolete time-space travel device. His only company has been Sadie, the maniacal computer support system of the Gogomobil, and ill-tempered Fafnir, the family dog. Fafnir dies from time to time, and is reconstituted and revivified by Sadie, whose technology is imperfect, resulting in some grotesque incarnations including a talking bowl of borscht. By the time the action of the story begins, Fafnir has taken on a vaguely humanoid appearance and the name King Dredle.

Also told or sung by Blind Grapefruit: Earlier, this scene has taken place: Irvinge has stopped in for a root beer at a roadside establishment run by Sid, an amorphoid fleshopod. The Gogomobil, apparently abandoned by its last owner, is in the parking lot. The boy Irvinge and Fafnir take refuge in the Gogomobil, and moments later an enormous gray and lethal presence manifests itself in the parking lot. It is Shdark, the loan shark.

"Dear God!" Sid whimpers.

"How's business?" Shdark says in a terrifying whisper.

"Oh please don't kill me," the fleshopod says, getting right to the point.

"Am I to understand that you haven't got twelve thousand six hundred and fifty zlotys for me?" asks the shark. He is motionless except for the regular undulations of his gill slits.

Sid looks for some sign of pity in the eyes of the shark, like huge round windows into nothingness.

"I've got six thousand," Sid says, "Somebody has been kidnapping the customers."

The sizable fleshopod is dwarfed by Shdark, who appears to be a great deal larger than a Greyhound bus.

"I'm sorry to hear that, really I am. You want to get ready now?"

"Please don't do it," Sid begs, "Take the six thousand. Let me live."

"I will take the six thousand," Shdark says, "but as to letting you live--well, Sid, I like you, really I do--and I'd like to let you live, but consider what that would do to my reputation. I'm trying to build a reputation."

"Oh Shdark, you've got a beautiful reputation," the fleshopod blubbers; "everybody hates and fears you."

"It's nice of you to say that," the shark whispers, "but, you see, that's the whole point. If I should fail to cause you to die in horrible agony, word might get around. People talk, Sid, they really do. What would happen to my business if I didn't make an example of you? It isn't my actual cruelty and viciousness that matters-- it's the perception of my cruelty and viciousness. People would say that I let you off and pretty soon . . . well, there's no point going on like this, really there isn't. But I tell you what--and don't let this get around--I'm going to kill you really fast. You won't feel a thing. Now don't say that Shdark never did anything for you. Ready?"

"Wait!" Sid shouts.

"Wait?" The shark waits.

"I'll give you the stand!"

"I get that anyway. I'll sell it to another schmuck like you."

"How about a space-time machine? A good space-time machine is worth forty, fifty thousand. I'll give you a space-time machine for the difference."

"Let's see it."

"There! It's there!"

"The Gogomobil? It's a piece of shit."

"No it's not! It's a classic! Look at the lines!"

"It hasn't got any lines. It's a piece of shit."

"You can get thirty thousand for it."

"I can allow you six thousand--that will leave you six hundred fifty shy."

"What will you do to me for that?"

"Let's see . . . for anything over five hundred, you have to die, but I like you, Sid, I really do--so here's what I'll do. I'll take the Gogomobil, and the six thousand, and you can owe me the six fifty at triple interest payable next time . . . and I'll bite off your head. Deal?"

"Deal!" the fleshopod says.

Minutes later, Shdark, with the Gogomobil containing Irvinge and Fafnir in his gullet, along with a fair-sized chunk of Sid, is making his way through infinity.

"That ignorant fucking fish," Sid chortles to himself, "that was my ass he bit off, and he never knew the difference."

29

BOOK ONE

The scene shifts: The parking lot of the Great
Discount Pharmacy. We learn the story of a family of Reptilian Roscoes which come to the Great
Discount Pharmacy, developing through two or
three generations, covering their arrival in the
parking lot, and their struggle to find a parking space, death, birth, maturation, and death—
then parking. We come to know Lamialeh, a scaly,
lidless darling and Irvinge's logical love.

Shdark arrives and disgorges the Gogomobil,
which in turn disgorges Irvinge, now grown to
manhood, and King Dredle. Also appearing is the
fragment of fleshopod which has shared the gullet of Shdark, has reconstituted itself, and
needless to say is a real asshole. There's nothing nice about this amorphoid fleshopod, who is

more than a brother to Sid (who will turn up later).

There is a dispute about the ownership of the Gogomobil, which Irvinge settles on the spot by killing Shdark neatly. This is a lucky stroke on Irvinge's part--a one-in-a-million long shot. Ordinarily Shdark would have made moo shu pork out of Irvinge, but somehow he is dispatched with a blow to his most vital ganglion.

Killing Shdark ruins his chances of making progress with Lamialeh, whom he has just glimpsed, and desires. Her upright family-- fairly stiff-necked, considering they're more or less snakes or lizards--will never approve of a warm-blooded ruffian like Irvinge.

BOOK TWO

Ratner, father of Irvinge, turns up. He does not
know Irvinge is there. Irvinge does not know
Ratner is there. Both have altered so much that
it is doubtful they would recognize one another
if they met. Of course they will meet, and
instantly resolve to kill one another, being
father and son.

Ratner is in a unique position, having worked
his way from a destitute stiff-seeker to a person of immense power. He has become an advisor
to the one repository of actual power in this
cosmos, J. Chronos Malfruddin, Chairman of the
Board, and owner of the Great Discount Pharmacy
Management Corporation. People grovel, invoke
his name, and (literally) kiss the ass of his
image, which is everywhere.

Irvinge is in love with Lamialeh, who may feel cold-blooded stirrings for him, but is forbidden to associate with him. Sid is en route. Events are brewing.

The greatest good throughout this time-space universe is the acquisition of halvah, more precious than gold, and conferring status on its possessor.

It is believed by simple folk that J. Chronos Malfruddin sits behind an enormous desk carved of solid halvah, and rests on a halvah bed at night.

Blind Grapefruit sings of the coming of Sid in search of his ass, the battle between Irvinge and the associates of Shdark, and the dreamy delights of Lamialeh's forked tongue and unwavering gaze.

A Gypsy caravan comes silently into the parking lot one dark night. By morning, there is a whole encampment, with trees, horses, grass, kettles bubbling over fires, quaint Gypsy songs, and quaint Gypsy cooking.

Right away, they steal Irvinge. This particular tribe of Gypsies starts life at about 160 pounds, so to them, Irvinge is a cute little pisher, and they treat him as such. His outrage, insistence that he's twenty-five years old, and attempts to run off, endear him to them all the more.

Novaleen, the Gypsy queen, takes a special fancy to little Irvinge, and clumsily pierces Irvinge's ear and fits him with a magical earring which has the power to make its wearer crafty and devious, qualities which Irvinge has lacked until now.

The earring can't be removed while the wearer still lives.

This is not a problem for Ratner, who having been told of the earring by King Dredle, who just dropped by to cadge some potato-skin soup, intends to get it. Ratner still does not know that Irvinge is his son, despite the singing of Blind Grapefruit, who has been telling the whole story. Ratner, like everyone else, ignores Grapefruit.

Ratner commissions Snake-piss, a freelance thug, to procure the earring.

But Novaleen learns of Ratner's intentions from King Dredle, in exchange for boiled pig tripe, and protects Irvinge--to an extent--by turning him into a werewolf.

This is accomplished by the nastiest kind of procedure, part magic, part ceremony, part infection. It makes it less likely that Snake-piss will be able to harm Irvinge--and it also addresses another problem the tribe has been having.

Larry, the tribe's usual werewolf, has become unpredictable. He's become less of an asset than a horrible liability.

Something that Novaleen had failed to make clear to Irvinge is that there can't be two were-wolves in the Gypsy band, at least not for very long. Irvinge will have to kill him.

Larry is a nice sort of fellow--a little depressed. He sits all day, stirring his pot of

ear-goulash and singing the old songs. He's
bored with lycanthropy.

But this doesn't mean he'd hesitate to tear
anyone to pieces if aroused.

Irvinge, made crafty and subtle by the magic
earring, decides not to kill Larry--certainly
not until he can get better odds. Novaleen and
most of the traditional Gypsies are waiting for
Irvinge to make his move and write a chapter in
the history of the tribe--which is made up mostly of this kind of thing. Blind Grapefruit sings
it.

Irvinge, however, is preoccupied with a plan
to abduct and ravish Lamialeh, his Reptilian
Roscoe love--or potential love.

King Dredle is to help with the abduction.

Lamialeh wants to be abducted.

However, King Dredle, for a consideration,
tips off Ratner, who has influence with Lamialeh's father, Siii.

When Irvinge shows up to abduct, Snake-piss is
waiting for him. In the darkness, Irvinge mistakes Snake-piss for Lamialeh, and pounces,
thinking to do a little preabduction warming up.

The sounds of struggle awaken Siii, who fangs
Irvinge on the leg, causing his instant death.

While dead, Irvinge is unable to prevent
Snake-piss from removing the earring, and ear.

King Dredle shoulders Irvinge's one-eared
corpse, and takes it around with him, possibly
in hopes of seeing it restored to life. He seeks
advice from the odd shaman, chiropractor, sur-
geon, and prostitute, usually in blind-pig
saloons and brothels.

BOOK THREE

Ratner receives the earring from Snake-piss. He
wears it, and also Irvinge's ear, still attached. Snake-piss suggests that Ratner might
also wish to acquire Lamialeh. Now that she's
been ravished, Siii is willing to part with her
at a reasonable rate. Ratner agrees, and commissions Snake-piss to negotiate for her. He
begins his negotiations by ravishing her a second time, reasoning that this will bring the
price down further.

Larry, the werewolf, views it as his responsi-
bility to get the earring back for Novaleen--
also Irvinge's ear for his own purposes, and if
possible, Ratner's ear too, as a bonus.

Irvinge is still dead. King Dredle is schlep-
ping his cadaver around--but sometimes mislays
it, leaves it out in the weather, allows it to

be used as a temporary article of furniture, an anchor, a door--all of which take a toll. Irvinge is getting a bit worn.

One of the fellows dead Irvinge runs into is Shdark. Shdark feels he has been humiliated by Irvinge. He is going to have to take revenge. Irvinge tries to avoid him.

Lamialeh is delivered to Ratner.

Larry has traced Ratner.

Shdark has caught up with Irvinge in the realm of the dead.

Ratner is about to ravish Lamialeh.

Lamialeh is all for it.

Larry is about to get back Novaleen's earring with a two-ear bonus.

Shdark pounces.

Ratner pounces.

Larry pounces.

Lamialeh, in an access of passion, returns Ratner's pounce, and not only ravishes him back, but ravishes Larry before he gets away. This works a change on Larry, making him even less dependable than before.

Shdark is doing horrible things to Irvinge.

King Dredle arrives with Irvinge's corpse, just as all these events are taking place.

At the same moment, Sid shows up. We know about Sid, too--but exactly what he wants or will do is not clear yet.

Irvinge is still dead. He doesn't care for it. Mostly he sits around with other departed, playing Michigan rummy.

Sid, the amorphoid fleshopod, approaches the parking lot on his endless quest for what may

have been the best part of him. Said portion has
regenerated into a dynamic villain, quite different from Sid, who is a good skate, if a little hideous, slimy, carbuncular, and randomly
tufted.

It's certain that Sid is going to be disap-
pointed or worse when he catches up to himself.
His alter-tuchas, Keester Button, is truly nasty
and generally feared. He's the butt of nobody's
joke.

Sid meets two men of wisdom, Herk and Bare.
They too are traveling to the parking lot and,
they hope, the Great Discount Pharmacy, with a
purpose in mind. They have heard of a recently
dead hero whom they suspect of being a major
religious figure, and they seek his shrine. It's
Irvinge, of course, but never identified by
name. Blind Grapefruit may know that the god-
hero is our hero, but the active characters
never quite make the connection.

Herk and Bare are persuasive and charismatic,
and Sid experiences what spiritual awakening an
amorphoid fleshopod might experience, and post-
pones his own quest to throw in with them.

They take refuge in a lean-to beside a puddle
on the outskirts of the lot, which is also the
temporary home of King Dredle. They do not suspect that one of the roof supports is the ultimate relic of the faith they are evolving.

In the realm of the dead, Shdark catches up
with Irvinge and begins a refined and, given
where and what they are, endless torment.

Malfruddin has appointed Ratner Principal
Inquisitor, in lieu of concrete payment for

Lamialeh, whom he has installed as a vestal in an establishment said to be a stepping-stone to the Great Discount Pharmacy. (There is, it now turns out, a body of opinion to the effect that the Great Discount Pharmacy can only be attained through religious exercise.) Nomenclature aside, it does not differ much from the other brothels. Lamialeh is happy in her work, but sometimes misses Irvinge.

Ratner, wishing to get on, vigorously extirpates false cults, and levys heavy fines. He also fines heavy Levys.

Shdark finds new and wonderful nasty things to do to Irvinge.

Herk, Bare, Sid, and King Dredle are preaching a confused gospel. What they have to say is sufficiently devoid of meaning that no one can find a point with which to take issue. It so happens that rumors are rife to the effect that the Great Discount Pharmacy does not exist--an unheard-of expression of nihilism, which has the entire parking lot in turmoil. In the unsettled circumstances, the doctrine which Herk and Bare and company are putting forth is accepted by a fair number of the inhabitants.

Naturally, anybody who has much of anything (which includes, and is more or less limited to, Malfruddin) would want this sort of doctrine squelched. Ratner is gathering information and about to come down hard on these apostates.

In the netherworld, Shdark is getting bored. He pauses in tormenting Irvinge to think up a new and more entertaining punishment.

Keester Button, that asshole, is foreshadow-
ing his way toward a confrontation with innocent
Sid, the amorphoid fleshopod, who is currently
just an ordinary religious fanatic.

Lamialeh has been converted to the fledgling
religion, never suspecting that the departed
savior is really her onetime sweetie, Irvinge.
She has left the quasi—state-religious establishment, and is alternately plying her craft,
preaching the gospel according to Sid, and
enjoying ecstatic religious states in the
streets.

Shdark figures out a new amusement: killing
Irvinge. This he does--and is delighted that it
works. Irvinge, killed in deadster-land is pro-
pelled back into the realm of the living--the
parking lot--where he is killed by Ratner. This
shoots him back to the other world, where Shdark
is delighted to dispatch him again. And he goes
right back to where Ratner is--and gets killed
some more. And to Shdark, who kills him. This
goes on for quite a while.

Meanwhile, as usual, no one recognizes Irvinge
as the subject of the current theological dispute.

The populace is distracted by Keester Button's
assault on Sid. This turns out to be a struggle
of such energy that it more or less brings to a
halt everything else that's going on. Thus, on
one of Irvinge's round trips from Hades, Ratner
neglects to kill him, and Lamialeh mistakes him
for a trick, and in effect rescues him.

Mutually destroying one another, Sid and

Keester are reunited in death, and Herk and Bare make a few last-minute changes in the script which serve to make of Sid the prophet and savior. The inhabitants of the parking lot generally accept this, and the new religion is codified, and immediately driven underground by Ratner's Inquisition. However, there is reason to believe that the existing social order (such as it is) will be eroded from underground by secret practitioners. Revolution and dangerous ideas are festering.

BOOK FOUR

Affection blossoms again between Lamialeh and Irvinge, and they go off to compare mammalian and reptilian modes of love.

Ratner recalls that he hasn't killed Irvinge for some time, and makes a note to get back to it when he has a chance.

Malfruddin ponders that he is going to have to organize terror on a grand scale, as turbulent times are coming.

Irvinge and Lamialeh set up housekeeping. There are the usual problems with relatives. Hers are reptiles. They take a dim view of Irvinge. Irvinge's only relative is Ratner, his father (unknown to both of them), who periodically tries to kill him.

Irvinge himself has misgivings about his interspecies relationship, but in the beginning, he is a slave to Lamialeh's forked tongue and limpid, lidless eyes. Later, love tends to cool, especially after sundown when Lamialeh drops about twenty degrees and becomes sluggish. She also tends to be hard to live with when she's shedding her skin.

Irvinge, his former celebrity as the killer of Shdark and his near-elevation to demigod forgotten, has all he can do to struggle for a few crumbs of halvah, and he has, perhaps instinctively, taken on his father's old trade of freelance disposer of the dead.

King Dredle is on hand, and from time to time helps Lamialeh revive her old trade—but never when Irvinge is around.

The underground cult, which had begun when Irvinge was dead, continues to exist, and is transforming to a movement against the forces of organized repression.

Lamialeh gives birth. This gives rise to many utterances on Irvinge's part to the effect of how sharper than a serpent's tooth, etc. The kids are a cold-blooded lot.

Further familial complications arise when King Dredle discovers that Irvinge is the son of Ratner, and undertakes to bring the two together. They meet, neither sure if it's to be a family reunion or murder. Ratner waxes philosophical about Irvinge's scaly darling, whom he knows pretty well himself. They part with expressions of affection, each resolving to kill the other one when an opportunity presents itself.

Meanwhile, Malfruddin is preparing to make a major evil move.

Banditry, internecine war, expeditions to find the Great Discount Pharmacy (never successful), arrivals, and departures keep life in the parking lot interesting.

Irvinge, fed up with reptilian domesticity, finally leaves home. He also has lost his taste for the Byzantine political doings, and tangled web of underground religious and revolutionary movements. He moves into the Gypsy camp, and spends most of his time with Larry, the werewolf.

Shdark is secretly resurrected from the dead, and is kept under wraps by Malfruddin. Something is brewing.

Malfruddin makes his move. With plenty of muscle, including Shdark, who works for him now, he makes to enslave everyone. He succeeds. A period of abject slavery opens. Everyone is put to work building an enormous structure, which dwarfs sphinx and pyramids, and all the wonders of all the worlds. This is to surpass the Great Discount Pharmacy.

Many now wonder openly if the Great Discount Pharmacy ever existed--and are punished in ghastly ways for their expressions of doubt, but mostly for using breath for purposes other than Malfruddin's.

Only the freedom-loving Gypsies, and Irvinge with them, manage to evade Malfruddin's expanded Goon Squad, and escape working on the project, known as the "erection," partly because of its aspect.

Blind Grapefruit, now grown portly and known as Lardbelly, has sold out to Malfruddin and sings work songs, carries tales, and exhorts his fellows to work on the erection.

Ratner, who is making a fortune removing corpses from the work site, is approached by King Dredle, who persuades him to lead a band of rebels who live in the badlands, where the Dumpsters are, and harass Malfruddin's goons. After a battle with the Gypsy band on a fairly grand scale, the two renegade groups treat for peace, and join forces. Thus, Irvinge and Ratner are finally united, whereupon during a skirmish, Ratner is swallowed, Jonah-like, by Shdark, and lives, a prisoner, inside the fish.

This gives Irvinge even more cause to hate Shdark and desire vengeance. Also he wants to get Ratner out of Shdark's intestines.

Lamialeh, now old and blind and wise, turns up, with some of Irvinge's children, all grown mansnakes.

Irvinge's family is now restored--except Ratner--who nonetheless projects utterances telepathically from somewhere north of Shdark's gallbladder.

Novaleen dies, and with Ratner closed up inside the shark, Irvinge is the logical leader of the combined Gypsy band, Ratner's followers, and various other groups and individuals, who have formed together.

BOOK FIVE

Conflict with Malfruddin is inevitable.

The erection is nearing completion.

News comes that a party of crab people from the Galaxy of Twilbstein have found the actual Great Discount Pharmacy.

The order maintained by Malfruddin through force and terror breaks down. Everybody goes there.

It surpasses all descriptions which have gone before. However, instead of tranquilly taking in the pleasures offered, the vast and endless unruly and desperate mob, having been enslaved for years by Malfruddin, and having, for the most part, no halvah credits with which to enjoy the Great Discount Pharmacy, trash and plunder the place.

This takes years. It amounts to warfare. Defense of parts of the Great Discount Pharmacy by mercenaries and merchant princes, feuds and fallings-out between allies, and the occasional invasion from groups, peoples, species, and entities hitherto not heard from, retard the destruction. But it does go forward, little by little.

Irvinge, who is now old, leads many raids, and lays waste to vast areas of the Great Discount Pharmacy. Irvinge is constantly looking for Shdark. Lamialeh dies. Many of Irvinge's scaly sons die. King Dredle dies, and Irvinge, remembering that King Dredle had once schlepped his, Irvinge's, cadaver through much of the book, returns the favor and always carries King Dredle's corpse into battle--used as a shield.

The Great Discount Pharmacy wars drag on for years.

Finally, Irvinge finds Shdark. Their conflict takes place on a number of planes, and largely in realms to which other beings never go. While they are hacking and chewing on one another's physical selves, they discuss a wide range of esoteric topics. All other activity ceases for the many days it takes for Irvinge and Shdark to work out which of them is to die. Ratner is still living in Shdark's kishkes, and adds his comments and advice.

Shdark dies hard. It takes pages. It's a little like the death of the Buddha.

When Shdark is finally done dying, neither Great Discount Pharmacy nor parking lot is viable. Many, if not most, are dead themselves, and the only object not reduced to minirubble is Malfruddin's partial erection, which casts a weird shadow.

Complete desolation. Irvinge and King Dredle, who is still dead, reflect on the events of their lives. Ratner has taken over the role of Blind Grapefruit (later Lardbelly), who was destroyed in the wars.

The remaining residents of the parking lot bide their time, cooking what and who they can find among the ruins.

Malfruddin emerges from the wreckage. No one moves against him. The lust for carnage has been satisfied. The characters move about as Irvinge did in Book Two when he resided in the realm of death.

Gradually, inspired by Ratner, the survivors coalesce and bond into one group. They are all going off in search of the True Great Discount Pharmacy, reasoning that the one they trashed wasn't the true one or they couldn't have destroyed it.

With Irvinge leading them, and leaving Ratner behind, telling his stories to himself, they leave the site of the old parking lot, and begin their quest.

34

Milton Cramer received a thick manila envelope at work. It felt as though it might contain twenty-five or thirty pages, and was stiffened with two pieces of corrugated cardboard. The return address was that of Milo Levi-Nathan, and the package was insured for a thousand dollars and came special delivery, return-receipt-requested. Another manuscript. Milton got them all the time.

He had carried it in his hand, unopened, when he left the office, on his way to attend the Fight Fat Fight Failure meeting. He thought he might read it afterward while he ate his evening meal in some restaurant. He had it with him in the taxi. He remembered playing with it, spinning it, turning it over and over, juggling with it, scratching an itch with the corner of it, drumming on it with his fingers, and stroking it during the ride.

At some point, he forgot all about it. He had no recollection of the package, or where he had last seen it. It might have been left behind at the meeting room, but he had no intention of going back to inquire. Fight Fat Fight Failure was not the self-help organization for Milton. All the disparagement made him uneasy, and it was preferable to avoid the scene entirely. Besides, he was reasonably certain he had not had it with him when he arrived at the Bandag Metaphysical Foundation.

Most likely he had left it in the taxi, or it had slid off the seat and fallen into the gutter when he emerged from the taxi.

All this he thought two or three days later when he went to enter the next manuscript to arrive in the logbook kept for that purpose, noticed the receipt of Milo's on the line above, and remembered that he had carried the envelope out of the office, and that it was lost.

"These things happen," Milton thought.

Dear Milo—

Just a note to tell you that your latest submission is not for us. Sorry—that's just the way it goes sometimes. Please don't give up on us. We're still very strong on you as a writer!

Our mailroom folks will be sending it back to you shortly—I just wanted to get this note off to you as soon as possible.

Hang in there!

Milton

36

Gypsy Bill's Hungarian-American Cafeteria and Bakery was a large storefront, deeper than it was wide, with two rows of long tables from front to back. Along one side of the room were glass cases, behind which were shelves, displaying a variety of cakes and breads, also toothachingly sweet pastries with lurid pink icing, napoleons, jelly doughnuts (also known as bismarcks), crullers oozing custard and chocolate, Linzer tarts, bear claws, hazelnut crescents, and the stickiest of sticky buns. In the back were the kitchen and the bake-ovens, which doubled as meat roasters.

It was not a true cafeteria—Gypsy Bill himself, in a long apron, or the formidable Mrs. Bill took orders and waited on customers. In addition to roasted meats, the bill of fare might include dumplings, spaetzle, noodles, potatoes, borgelnuskies, and special red cabbage, dark, oily, and unidentifiably seasoned which was served with everything, and was alone worth the trip from anywhere. The coleslaw, too, was highly regarded by experts. But most famous, and most admired, was Gypsy Bill's "Evening in Budapest" brisket special, which had been known to bring on waking dreams, night sweats, and abrupt and inexplicable changes in the life courses of those who ordered it.

Ranged along the tables, under the flickering fluorescent lights, sat the customers, usually men, usually alone, some reading books, some reading complimentary copies of *The Flying Saucer News,* which Bill, a UFOlogist, provided. Others engaged in dreamy mastication fantasies while listening to the powerful nonstereo Grundig "Imperator" radiophonograph, c.1957, which alternated Bill's three favorite musical selections, the Tannhäuser Overture, the Haffner Symphony, and the theme from the movie *Lawrence of Arabia.*

Into this refuge, redolent of paprika, the very atmosphere of which was heavy with cholesterol and *gemütlichkeit,* came Laszlo Gegenschein, as he did every night.

Gegenschein paused just inside the door, and scanned the tables, looking for someone he knew. An enormous man, with negroid features and wearing a pin-striped suit, was sitting alone, reading a well-thumbed copy of Krafft-Ebing and conveying forkfuls of food to his mouth, in a state of greasy happiness.

"So, Plotkin, you like that better than *Patterns of Psychosexual Infantilism,* by Wilhelm Stekel?"

Dr. Alan Plotkin looked up, and saw the old man. "Hello, Mr. Gegenschein. Yes, you can't beat *Psychopathia Sexualis.* We're all in this book. Reads like a novel. Please, sit down."

"I don't want to interrupt your reading."

"Not at all. I'd enjoy your company. Sit."

Bill shuffled up. "I've got fresh borgelnuskies with a habañera sauce. You want?"

"I recommend it," Plotkin said.

"With extra cabbage," Gegenschein said. "And a glass of grape juice."

"Manolo! 'Nuskies, yuppie-style, double red, and a Welch's!" Bill bellowed. A stream of curses in Spanish emanated from the kitchen. "Your order will be up shortly, sir." Bill shuffled off.

"So, Doctor," Gegenschein asked. "What's new by you, healer of minds?"

"The usual thing," Plotkin said, buttering a hunk of kimmelwick. "Did you know that both the U.S. senators from this state are closeted gays?"

"I didn't know that," Gegenschein said.

"One of them's a client of mine. They're secretly married."

"Imagine that. A Republican and a Democrat."

"Well, mixed marriages sometimes work."

"I suppose."

"They have a lot in common, being in politics."

"Yeh."

A long pause.

"You know how it is," Plotkin yawned. "People come in. They talk to me. I talk to them. They go away. Other people come in. *They* talk to me. I sit. I listen. I give them a little advice. They usually ignore it. Some get a little better. Some get a little worse. I help them, I guess, to a certain extent."

"But you make a nice living."

"I'm satisfied. Ahhhhhhgh," Plotkin stretched, leaning back in his chair. "Bill, you got cherry cheesecake?"

"I got," Bill said. "And a coffee?"

"Please," the psychotherapist said.

"How's that boy you were telling me about—works in a publishing house?"

"Oh, Milton Cramer! His prognosis is no good. That fellow is cruising for a bruising. You get an instinct after a while, in this business. Something bad is going to happen to that guy—I can feel it in my bones."

"Milton Cramer, Milton Cramer—the name almost rings a bell," Gegenschein mused.

37

Milo and Linda came in, along with a burst of cold air, mixed with an emanation of their own robust energy, which read as heat. Never many hours from one of their bathtub frolics, they were pink and radiant, loofahed, steamed, and scrubbed to a fine polish, and beaming with good health and sexual contentment.

"I can't believe you didn't know about this place," Milo was saying. "Borgelnuskies every night, and the red cabbage is international."

"Milo, you know everything," Linda said, squeezing his arm.

"And the pastries are really authentic," Milo continued. "Oh, look! There's Dr. Plotkin!"

The ebullient couple approached the table where Plotkin and Laszlo Gegenschein were sitting, and stood there, emitting.

"Here's a young man who's going places," Plotkin said

to Gegenschein, rising and taking Milo's hand. "Laszlo Gegenschein, Milo Levi-Nathan. And this would be?"

"This is my colleague, Linda Kapustka," Milo said.

Hands were shaken all around. The others found themselves imitating Gegenschein's curt European salutation and slight bow.

"We won't intrude," Milo said.

"Not at all," Plotkin said. "Please join us, unless you'd prefer to be alone." Plotkin regarded Milo as a success story, almost unique among his clients, and was anxious to show off.

"If you're sure," Milo said exchanging glances with Linda. Milo wanted Linda to see him hold his own with intellectuals, and Linda, having never met any of Milo's friends, was naturally curious to know what her lover was like outside of work, the tub, and bed.

"We'd be honored, I assure you," Plotkin said.

Milo and Linda seated themselves, and ordered "Evening in Budapest" brisket specials, one apiece. Gypsy Bill went straight to the Grundig, put on his record of Brahms' Hungarian dances, and went to the kitchen to prepare the food himself.

"Milo Levi-Nathan? Another name I seem to have run across recently," Gegenschein mused.

"Levi is my original name," Milo said. "The Nathan is an add-on, my stepfather's. The Levi is a truncated name. It was Levinootzpiki. My people came from Blint."

"Blint!"

"You've heard of Blint? Most people haven't."

"Heard of it! Heard of Blint!" Gegenschein looked away with an indecipherable expression. "Yes. I have heard of Blint," he said slowly.

"Milo is an author," Plotkin said. "Any news on the publishing front?"

"I'm waiting to hear," Milo said brightly. "I sent in an outline for something with really fantastic potential."

"Blint," Gegenschein muttered to himself.

"Milo is a wonderful writer," Linda said.

"And what are you interested in, Linda?" Plotkin asked.

"I'm just a career girl," Linda said. She blushed. "As you probably know, I am employed by the Rubinstein's Orthodox Hot Dogs organization. I am in food preparation and sales, but I hope to move up to the managerial or executive level—and it is my dream to someday find a position in Sausage Design. It's a little-known fact that the great sausage manufacturers are constantly refining and improving their product. Armour, Oscar Mayer, Vienna, Hebrew National, and the Osterreicher Sausage Company of Green Bay, Wisconsin, all have staffs of highly trained professionals who work on both the nutritional and aesthetic aspects. I'm taking courses in culinary design, and I have some unusual ideas about things that could be done with kielbasa."

"Such a beauty," Gegenschein said.

"You're a lucky man, Milo," Plotkin said.

"I know," Milo said.

Linda blushed even redder and more becomingly.

38

Unto James Pembroke Palmer, M.D., known to his intimates as Peaches, and his wife, Elizabeth (Bingo) Harrison-Bennet Palmer, attorney-at-law, of Lake Forest, Illinois, a child was born. Christened Bentley Waughford Susan, at St. Stephen's Church, little Guppy, as she was called at home, was handed off to a qualified nurse-nanny, imported from England, at the age of eight weeks, when Mummsy returned to her work at the law firm.

Guppy was swaddled in the finest and softest cottons and wools, had a nursery equipped with visually stimulating and aesthetically correct decorations, a stereo system on which to hear the music of Erik Satie, and was engaged in structured play and exercise by her nanny, who had taken special training at the University of London College of Nursing.

Beginning at age two, Guppy attended play groups and dance classes organized for children of the fortunate, at four was enrolled in the preschool of the North Shore

French Academy, a bilingual school of impeccable credentials, and traveled with her parents to resorts and spas at home and abroad. On Sundays, she was taken to the zoo, and to the Art Institute of Chicago, where she was exposed to fine paintings and sculpture. She began ballet classes at six, and also did well in her riding lessons two afternoons a week.

Guppy's schoolwork was exemplary, she made great progress in French, and when she left the Academy to become a day pupil at the Wheaton Preparatory School, she was allowed to begin classes in Italian, and had special instruction in oil painting. Her parents contemplated taking advantage of Mount Holyoke's junior-year-abroad program and permitting Guppy to study in Rome.

Peaches and Bingo were alarmed by Guppy's sudden propensity to put on weight, which began in her high-school years. Both of them were serious about Good Food, and had nurtured an appreciation in their child of Serious Eating, which, of course, did not permit excess. When Guppy was nine, they had made a tour of cathedral towns in France, with reservations, made months in advance, at some of the greatest restaurant/shrines in civilization. The news that their daughter was sneaking off to gobble cheeseburgers with public-school children, and the discovery of wrappers from Snickers bars in her pockets, bewildered and depressed them.

Guppy willfully and sneakily undermined the best attempts, at school and at home, to initiate correct dietary habits. When it was discovered that she had been selling her fellow students items of clothing and tape cassettes to fund trips to McDonald's and the candy counter, her father arranged for treatment by some of his finest colleagues.

This was to no avail. In spite of medical advice and

treatment, visits to a behavior modification expert, and many tearful promises on Guppy's part, she continued to bulk up alarmingly. Her contours were already identical to those of Mrs. Shondar, the girl's phys. ed. teacher and field hockey coach at the Wheaton School. Peaches and Bingo were distracted.

At Mount Holyoke, free of parental watchfulness, Guppy, while maintaining a B-plus average, was free to expand exponentially. Her college roommate received the benefit of a second wardrobe—the clothes Guppy had brought with her, and had now outgrown. Guppy, clad in a few articles purchased in a local Army-Navy store, wandered the campus and the environs of South Hadley, Massachusetts, studying and eating. The formerly happy, not to say perfect, life of Peaches and Bingo had been all but ruined by the amplification of their only daughter. Bingo had waking nightmares of Guppy, home on vacation, appearing, shambling beside her in turned-up fatigue pants and field jacket, at the tennis courts. She began to shun conversations with her friends and colleagues for fear they would ask about her child. And Peaches, as a physician, had always hated and reviled fat people—and now his own offspring actually was one.

"Why does she hate us?" they asked one another.

In the end, there was nothing to do but pack her off to the clinic of the famous Dr. Unterwerfer in Potlatch, New York.

39

"It's for you, Doc." Joe held out the receiver.

Plotkin, carrying his mug of coffee, made his way to the pay phone.

"Hello?" he said.

"Plotkin-boy?"

"Mama?"

"Why haven't you called, Plotkin-boy? Why haven't you called your old mother?"

"I've been busy. Besides, I didn't know you had a phone."

"We've had this here telephone machine since nineteen and seventy-seven, and never once have you called. Your poor old mother has sat here, waiting, year after year, brokenhearted."

"So how come you didn't call me?"

"You don't care about us. You forgot all about us when you went off to that there university."

"That's not true, Mama."

"Oh, you sent us that coconut one time. And we still have that coconut. We didn't have the heart to eat it. It just sits there, on the mantelpiece, reminding us of our boy who went away."

"So how is everybody?"

"We're ailing, Plotkin-boy. Your Papa is ailing, your sisters are ailing, their kids are ailing, and your poor old Mama, that you don't even love, is ailing."

"Anything serious?"

"What do you care, you big, fat, intellectual son of a bitch? You think you're too good for your iggerant, poor white-trash family."

"Come on, Mama. You've got a degree from the University of Chicago, and so does Papa."

"Oh, yes. You've got a smart-ass answer for everything, don't you, Mr. Big-deal Alienist? I suppose you don't give a goddamn that the sow has a case of glanders, and that all we've had to eat for the last three months is what wild turkeys your Papa can shoot with his old arthritic fingers."

"Where does he find wild turkeys in Westchester County?"

"We none of us ever really liked you, do you know that?"

"I know that."

"But you're my only son, dammit, the fruit of my loins."

"Please, Mama! I'm eating!"

"Your Mama loves you."

"I love you too, Mama."

"And your Papa loves you."

"I love Papa, Mama."

"Of course, your sisters hate you."

"Yes, Mama."

"Come home, Plotkin-boy! Come home to Plotkin's Mountain."

"Goodbye, Mama."

Plotkin wiped a tear from his eye. "Good old Mama," he said.

40

A detailed account of Dr. Werner Unterwerfer's personal and professional history before coming to the United States was never listed in reference sources, and was therefore obscure. He had graduated from the Berliner Universität Horst Wessel Medizinische Fakultät, in 1941, and nothing official was noted in his record until his arrival in this country in 1954. Colleagues, hospital administrators, and patients preferred not to speculate about his past.

In conversation, he would make reference to his experience in the concentration camps, where he had evolved the theories for which he was celebrated. No one had ever asked, and almost no one had ever given thought to whether he had been *Sanitätsoffizier* or inmate—it was more comfortable to assume the latter, although as a rabid anticommunist, intemperate heterosexual, and certainly not a Gypsy or a Jew, it was hard to imagine what they'd have had him in there for.

For many years, Unterwerfer had been the last word in weight control. His private clinic, affiliated with St. Agatha's Hospital, was a prodigious moneymaker, and he was unquestionably Top Doctor, though his official status was adjunctive.

Unterwerfer had noticed, during his wartime experiences, that inmates of the camps had uniformly lost weight. He was not insensible to the negative aspects, and relatively short duration, of life in those places—but he came to certain conclusions which were remarkable, not to say astonishing.

Unterwerfer opined that, after execution and beatings, the main cause of death in the concentration camps was depression, brought on by the unpleasant attitude of the Nazi guards. Knowing they were hated, and generally condemned to death, lowered the prisoners' spirits and resistance to disease. However, some survived, even in such hostile conditions—and why was that?

Unterwerfer concluded it was the diet. Based on his belief, shared by many of his colleagues even then, that maximal thinness is the sovereign key to good health, he reasoned that the rapid bodily reduction of those held prisoner was a potentially good thing in most cases, and would have conferred a benefit, had the Nazis been less nasty.

Meticulous records of nutritional matters were kept, of course, and Unterwerfer made a point of collecting copies of these for his personal use. After the war, on a secluded *estancia* in South America, he studied this data, and refined his theory. His model for an ideal weight-reduction program was charmingly simple—the familiar thin gruel, potato-skin soup, and sawdust loaf of the camps, healthful exercise in the out-of-doors, regular hours, strict organization, but all administered by kindly Germans, rather than sadistic ones.

He got his chance to put his ideas into practice when a former colleague, Dr. Klaus Fassbender, a podiatrist, practicing in Potlatch, New York, sponsored Unterwerfer's application for admission to the U.S. as a displaced person.

Unterwerfer obtained local certification, and built a modest practice in Potlatch. In the early sixties he wrote and published a book, *You* Will *Lose Weight!* subtitled "The Afrika Korps Diet," a tenuous claim, supported by a photocopy of a brief personal note, of dubious provenance, from Erwin Rommel, commending Unterwerfer for his good work and alleging a satisfying weight loss based on his advice. The book was a runaway success, with forty-eight weeks on *The New York Times* best-seller list, and was the foundation of an empire of sorts.

The Unterwerfer clinic, occupying twenty acres, adjacent to St. Agatha's Hospital, had deluxe bungalows, an all-European staff, state-of-the-art sports facilities, and was attended by many famous and wealthy patients, whose privacy and safety were assured by the state-of-the-art barbed-wire fence and guard towers.

41

The Mei Ling was a Chinese restaurant in the old tradition. Redolent of roach powder and star anise, dark and commodious, there were lantern light fixtures with tassels, dragons everywhere, carved, painted, embroidered, printed on menus and napkins, glazed on crockery, black-lacquered wooden latticework between the booths, and ceramic tree-bark tiki glasses with simulated carved faces. The place was dense with chichi chinoiserie. Nathan Eng, and his father before him, and his father before him, had purchased every item listed in the Orientalia section of Goldberg's Restaurant Supply catalogue. And the waiters were authentic, dour, shuffling old men, in red jackets, brusque with newcomers and ingratiating to regulars.

Milton was a regular. Eng and the waiters loved him. His proportions were identical to those of the life-size carved wooden Hotei, which stood with arms upraised in a gesture of happy welcome, next to the cashier's station. A fat man is more precious than jade in a Chinese restaurant—a living good-luck charm, evidence of quality, and an omen of success.

When Milton arrived with Jennifer, a woman of matching globularity, Eng felt his soul rise up. He had been brooding about changes in pedestrian traffic wrought by the opening of a mall a few miles away. His own stupid cousin, Arthur, was coining money with an enterprise known as Mongolian Express—a tiny space seating only twenty, where everything was served on plastic-foam plates from trays of soggy food on a glassed-in steam table. "It's dreck!" Eng had told Arthur. But Arthur was doing twice Eng's business, with a staff of teenage part-timers. "Dreck makes money," Arthur had said. "You gonna argue with Walt Disney?"

"Mister Milton!" Eng said, smiling happily. "So good to see you—and the lady."

Eng himself seated Milton and Jennifer at the best table, a booth in a cubicle, almost a room. The dragon lantern cast a circle of light on the linen tablecloth. A bowl of fried noodles and two little dishes containing hot mustard and duck sauce were brought.

Jennifer eyed the noodles with dismay. "Um, if you don't mind," she said to Milton.

"Yes, of course," Milton said. To the waiter, "Please take the noodles away."

"It's just that one munches on them. And they're fried."

"Yes, yes," Milton said. "Chinese cuisine is excellent for dieters, if you avoid things like that."

"I know of a man who lost a hundred pounds, just by eating in Chinese restaurants."

"I can well believe it," Milton said.

"Oh, look!" Jennifer said, pointing to the menu. "They have a diet section! Prepared with scallions, garlic, ginger,

and wine! No oil, salt, sugar, cornstarch, or MSG! Is that
what you usually order?"

"Yes."

"How about we have the chicken and broccoli?"
Jennifer consulted an electronic calorie counter, like a
pocket calculator.

"Good choice," Milton said.

"Are you on any special food plan? I hate the word
'diet,' " Jennifer said.

Milton had dropped in at Rubinstein's the night before,
having first ascertained through the window that it indeed
was Milo's night off, and had consumed four Milwaukee
bratwurst sandwiches with spicy mustard and grilled
onions, two coffee milkshakes, and had engaged a person-
able and pneumatic blond server in light chitchat.

"I try to stay a little hungry," he said. "I eat more or
less what I like."

"The chicken and broccoli is OK, isn't it?"

"Oh, certainly."

"I tried the think slim–be slim thing. You know it? The
book was very good. But I couldn't seem to make it work
for me. I need more structure." Jennifer was dipping her
fingertip in the duck sauce, and sucking it delicately.

"Have you read *Diets Don't Work*?" Milton asked.

"Excellent book!"

"It was a best-seller. Over four hundred thousand
copies in print," Milton said.

"Of course, publishing is your business," Jennifer said.
Milton had told her on the way over.

"There's a sequel, you know: *Diets Still Don't Work*."

"I didn't know. I'll have to read it."

"I can lend you my copy," Milton said. "But the really
hot one is *The Very Last Diet Book You'll Ever Need*."

"Is it by the same author as *The Last Diet Book You'll Ever Need*? I read that one. I thought it was great."

The blanched chicken and steamed broccoli arrived. Milton and Jennifer smiled at one another synthetically. They began to pick at the tasteless food.

"You know what they do really well here?" Milton said. "Sweet and sour crispy sea bass."

"Really?" Jennifer enthused. "I haven't had my fish unit today. And I missed lunch."

"Waiter!" Milton called.

42

"What's the matter? You look lousy." Alan Plotkin was at his place of work, plying his craft, and knocking back a three-egg, three-cheese omelette with home fries well done, plenty of ketchup, a stack of whole wheat, and a mug of coffee, cream-no-sugar. His first client of the day was Milton Cramer, who significantly had ordered no more than a cup of tea.

"All this self-loathing and destructive behavior is getting me down," the wretched editor said.

"Uh-oh," Plotkin said, shaking pepper on his eggs. "Gonna be one of those mornings. What do you want to talk about first, the self-loathing or the destructive behavior?"

"I'm a monster," Milton said.

"Who isn't? Be more specific."

"I can't control what I eat!"

"What does that mean? You find yourself ordering

Spam and creamed spinach? You have an oatmeal fetish? What?"

"Last night, I met a woman."

"And you ate her? Where are you going with this?"

"We went to a Chinese restaurant."

"Which one?"

"Mei Ling."

"Good choice."

"This is a very nice woman. She's sort of heavy, too. I met her at that self-help group."

"Starve for Success?" Plotkin snorted. "I warned you about them—they're really sick."

"I just wanted to see for myself," Milton said. "I agree it's not for me, but it seems to help some of them."

"I can't understand it," Plotkin said. "If you gouge your own eyes out, or bash your head against a brick wall, after a while, someone will come and take you to a hospital, but those people are allowed to have public meetings."

"Anyway, after the meeting, we struck up a conversation. I liked her. I think she liked me. I invited her to supper."

"Sounds very pleasant."

"Wait. We get to the restaurant. She orders from the diet section."

"Diet section?"

"In the menu. They have a selection of diet foods."

"I never noticed."

"She's trying to lose weight. She thinks, for some reason, that I've got it together better than she has. I don't know—she looks upon me as more experienced, capable, wants me to take the lead."

"Sounds promising."

"So I took the lead, all right. Listen to what I got her to

eat. Sweet-and-sour crispy sea bass. Butterfly shrimp with bacon. Pork in black bean sauce. Four egg rolls, two apiece. Tangerine beef. Fried dumplings. Crab and bean curd soup. And six bowls of Jell-O."

"Well, they're little bowls," Plotkin said.

"In the end, she was looking at me as though I'd raped her."

"Maybe she was just glassy-eyed from eating all that."

"No, she hates me—and she should."

"Why do you say that? She should have been grateful to you, after a wonderful meal like that, and if she was able to move, have given herself to you."

"I violated her."

"Oh, she did give herself to you."

"No, I violated her trust. I made her eat."

"I really doubt that. Urged her, maybe—but that's just common politeness."

"It's tragic," Milton said. "Here are two intelligent people, with a lot to offer one another, and instead of communicating, we just sat there, eating—wrapped up, insulated by fat—insulated from possible feelings."

"Oh, no! Not this idiocy again! Has someone told you, or did you read somewhere, that being fat is supposed to be padding against unwanted or frightening emotions or relationships?"

"Yes. Something like that."

"So, if you're fat, it's because you need a barrier between yourself and emotionally threatening stuff?"

"Yes. Isn't that so?"

"No. It is not so. The reason you're fat is that you're fat. That's all. You're fat for the same reason people have big noses, or red hair. It's one of the shapes people come in. It doesn't necessarily *mean* anything."

"But what about all the excessive eating?"

"We have to eat like that, with big bodies like these. It would be excessive if you were a little shrimp. For a fat person, it's normal."

"Oh yes, I forgot. We had shrimp balls too."

"They do them great there, don't they?"

"So what are you saying? You think maybe she doesn't hate me?"

"I don't know. I'm starting to hate you for being such a boring putz—but women are more tolerant. Why don't you call her up and find out?"

"You think I should?"

"Why not? Give her a couple of days to get over that meal, and ring her. What can it hurt?"

"Maybe you're right. But, really, I should do something about my weight, shouldn't I?"

"Jeezus!"

43

Wiley Sinclair was preparing supper in his small, cluttered room. On the corner of his table, he had set up a propane stove, which looked like a metal toolbox. He kept the stove under his bed when not in use, next to the cardboard carton of cooking utensils, which he washed in the tiny sink in the communal bathroom down the hall.

He opened a can of generic house-brand corned-beef hash with his Swiss Army knife, and dumped the contents into his skillet. While he moved the hash around with the fork he'd eat it with out of the pan it was now cooking in, set on a folded newspaper, he read in a book printed in thick Fraktur characters. It was a German book, printed more than a hundred years before. The pages were thick, and densely covered with type. It had lost its cover, and was now bound in cardboard and dirty masking tape.

There were a few more books in Sinclair's room—mostly foreign-language dictionaries, and a paperback copy of

Dracula by Bram Stoker. There were also a number of notebooks—the spiral kind with utilitarian brown covers. The notebooks were arranged in a row, on top of the dresser that came with the room. They were marked on their covers with marking pen: "Short Essays"; "Dacoits"; "Witchcraft in 19th Century Midwest"; "Leopard Societies of West Africa"; "Modern Lycanthropy"; "Voudoun in Urban America"; "Human Spontaneous Combustion"; "Extraterrestrial Visitors in Eastern Europe"; "Blint I"; "Blint II"; "Blint III."

44

The East-West Arterial consisted of two three-lane one-way roads, a block apart, which cut through the heart of a formerly desirable neighborhood of one- and two-family homes with big backyards. Now the inhabitants heard the roar of traffic continuously, and mercury-vapor lights created a sort of polar summer effect when night fell. The area between the two roads was by way of achieving the highest domestic violence and suicide rates in the city, property values had plummeted, and the houses were already showing signs of neglect—gardens overgrown, paint peeling, derelict cars parked in the street, and large discarded articles on front lawns.

But this sacrifice was as nothing compared to the benefit conferred by the Arterial. Fast access to and from the suburbs, and more important, to and from the Grand Mall.

The Grand Mall, which completely supplanted yet

another residential and commercial district, once an independent incorporated village, was the last word in modern retail planning and design. Vast thousands of wildly enthusiastic shoppers visited the mall 365 days a year, between eight A.M. and eleven P.M. Two and three levels high, with a magnificent atrium, splendid in shining chromium and tinted glass, with transepts, clerestories, and the great apse containing a top-of-the-line Sears, the Grand Mall served the aesthetic, not to say spiritual, as well as the commercial needs of the people.

Emporia of every conceivable kind were arrayed in the mall. All the major department stores were represented, specialty shops specializing in every specialty, an embarrassment of inexpensive food concessions, including the popular Mongolian Express, and a Cinema 25, which had precipitated the failure of every movie house in a fifty-mile radius.

Here, also, was Circumferus Maximus, the big man's shop, the source of fashionable garments for the diametrically disadvantaged and the altitude challenged. Here one could acquire colorful shirts made of one hundred percent virgin acrylic, trousers up to size 72 and with a fifty-inch inseam. Here was the last place on earth offering the classic white patent-plastic belt, and matching perforated shoes, with tassels, the Filipino mabuhey shirt, in eye-catching pastel colors, and the venerable leisure suit. And here, browsing through a rack of sweaters, from a factory in southeast Asia, the diminutive workers of which must have had strange dreams indeed of the quintuple-extra-large end-users of their product, was Milton Cramer. And here, contemplating a tropical-motif bathrobe large enough to envelop both himself and his knackwurst-loving lover, Linda, was Milo Levi-Nathan.

The two literary men espied one another, exchanged greetings, fell into conversation, and adjourned to Mongolian Express for a cup of hot *cha* and a half-dozen egg rolls apiece.

"I have to tell you," Milo said. "I was pretty devastated that you didn't like my outline."

Milton's disk drive whirred for a couple of seconds. He had forgotten all about the thick manila envelope and his letter to the author, who sat across from him, squeezing duck sauce from a tiny plastic pouch onto egg roll number three.

File found. "Look, Milo, anything you write is going to be good. I have to straddle a line between acting in my company's commercial interest, and being a friend of Art. It just wasn't something we felt we could do justice to in the marketplace. And we could be wrong. I urge you to submit it elsewhere."

"So you liked it?"

"Sure, I liked it. I like everything you write."

"You know, I still haven't gotten the manuscript back."

Whirr. "Our mailroom has been screwing up lately. And you know what the Postal Service is like these days. I'll run a check on it."

"I was really sure I had something there."

"Milo, it can take a long time to find your voice as a writer. These early efforts are never a waste. I've got a lot of confidence in you."

"Really?"

"You think I talk like this to all the writers who submit stuff to us? You've got real talent."

"It's so important to hear you say that," Milo said. "I'm normally a pretty optimistic guy, but sometimes, I wonder if I'm ever going to get my career started."

"Look," Milton said, feeling a twinge of almost-guilt. "This may not be something you want—but at least I could pay you a little something. Would you be willing to do a little freelance editorial work?"

"I don't know," Milo said. "What's involved?"

"Just doing a little first reading, and writing a few pages of comment for me. The money's ridiculous, but it's good experience—could help you develop a sense of what's marketable."

"I just read it, and . . ."

"Just read it, and write a couple of pages, boiling it down to essentials, and, of course, add your opinions. I have a lot of confidence in your taste."

"Well . . . sure. I'd like to try it."

"Good, I'll send you a manuscript. I've got one that needs reading. Nonfiction. We do a certain amount of stuff about sasquatch, evidence of extraterrestrial visitors to ancient civilizations, the Loch Ness monster— that sort of thing. This is about mysterious events in Outer Transylvania or some such place in Eastern Europe."

"Interesting. My ancestors came from there."

"So did mine. Changing the subject, have you ever tried to do anything about your weight?"

"You mean go on a diet? Sure. Lots of times. I mean, I'm pretty comfortable, and my current girlfriend says she likes me just the way I am—but I wouldn't mind shedding a few pounds, if only to get away from the kind of money they charge us to cover ourselves in polyester."

"You're right. Aren't the prices ruinous? So what kinds of diets have you tried?"

"Oh, all kinds. My mother subscribes to a lot of magazines that deal with nutrition. I had a lot of success with the pizza and chocolate-cupcake diet. It's based on the idea that you pick a couple of things you really like, and just eat those—in moderate quantities."

"You had success? Did you lose a lot of weight?"

"No. But I stayed with it the longest."

45

Milton missed Natalie. Although he'd only spoken to her a few times, she was the closest thing to a friend he'd had in the place. Anyway, she was friendly. The other residents were civil but abstracted. People tended to look off into the distance while one was talking to them, and conversation drifted abruptly into silence. She had been the only one to look him in the eye, and now, apparently, she was growing up in an affluent suburb, developing good eating habits, with no recollection of who she had been, or any notion that she had heretofore been anybody, and certainly no memory of Milton.

Milton decided to attend a meeting of the Teatime T-group, or Daze of Atonement, which met afternoons at four. A dozen or so chairs were arranged in a circle in the casino, and five or six rotund residents shuffled in, got themselves a plastic-foam cup of coffee or tea, and took their places, keeping a chair's width between themselves and the next participant. Charlie, in a turtleneck and tweed jacket, was the facilitator. He also affected a pair of horn-rims and a pipe.

"Welcome, vitality-challenged persons. This is where we unburden, share, validate, and adjust to our new status as the alternatively animated. We do not judge, we only listen, acknowledge, relate, and nurture. Each of us has her or his story to tell, and a stiff's a stiff for a' that."

The members of the group, all female, except for Milton, avoided eye contact, sipped at their cups, and said nothing. Charlie chewed on his pipe, which had no tobacco in it.

"Who's going to start?" Charlie asked. "How about you, Estrella?"

Estrella, a tidy, round grandmother type, cleared her throat delicately. "I hated my children. I resented having to carry them, was frightened and disgusted when I gave birth to them, was bored taking care of them—and as their personalities emerged, I found I did not like them. My greatest fear is that they will die and come here, and I'll be forced to associate with them."

"Good, Estrella!" Charlie said. "Wonderful job! Get those humiliating confessions out! Any comments, gang?"

"I think it was very brave of you to share with us, Estrella."

"I personally can relate to this, and I feel much stronger for having heard you."

"Estrella, maybe they just weren't nice children. That happens."

Milton felt he should add a comment. "I don't think my mother liked me." Sharp glances from everyone, and a palpable chill. "And I turned out all right. . . ." He trailed off. The group members shifted their bodies slightly, turning away from him.

Charlie summed up. "Estrella, you aren't required to actually *like* your children. You gave them life—that's plenty. They owe you eternal gratitude, and God forgives you, even though you did nothing wrong."

The women closest to Estrella on either side leaned toward her, hugged and patted her, while the others made comforting sounds.

"Thanks," Estrella sniffled. "I feel a lot better."

The atmosphere was warming, Milton noticed, though none of the warmth appeared to be directed toward him.

"Who wants to go next?" Charlie asked, settling back in his chair.

"I'm afraid what I did was worse," another woman said. "I messed with my children's minds, turned them against each other, withheld love until they did what I wanted, undermined their self-esteem, insulted them for my own amusement, and before I died, I gave strangers the money my husband left me, just so they couldn't inherit it."

"That's very perceptive, Faith, and well expressed," Charlie said. "You show real insight. Who's got a comment?"

"Did you call them little bastards?" Estrella asked.

"Yes."

"So did I. Did you complain that you wished you'd never had kids?"

"All the time."

"Me too."

"Excuse me," another woman said. "I think, Faith didn't like her children, either—just like Estrella."

"So, if you didn't like them, you didn't like them. It's

not your fault. You can't control who you like and who you don't."

"Good work, group," Charlie said. "Faith, you don't have to worry about a thing. You were a good mother."

Billie, a bouncy woman with a winsome drawl, was next. "I didn't have any children, but I used and manipulated my friends. I pretended to be shy and weak, and encouraged people to take care of me and do all sorts of things for me. I solicited advice, and got others to do my work. I made a point of never picking up a lunch check, or even putting a dime in a parking meter for another person. Whenever I felt I didn't need somebody anymore, I'd turn on them, and become derisive and abusive."

"What you're saying, Billie," Charlie said, "is that you gave your friends months and years of happiness in feeling protective and virtuous, against maybe one moment of withering realization that you were actually a shit—as which of us is not?"

"When you look at it that way . . . ," Billie said.

"You were a first-rate person. Now let's hear from Milton."

"I used to be an editor in a publishing house."

"Euwww!"

"I'd sort of encourage writers I had no intention of publishing. When I did publish someone, I'd mess with their minds. I used to enjoy the feeling of power. The writing meant everything to them, and really nothing to me. I could really make those authors sweat."

"That's how you got your kicks, you miserable bastard?"

"One time, I lost a manuscript before I'd read it, and instead of telling the author, I pretended I thought it wasn't publishable."

"You're disgusting."

"How come he's here instead of burning in Hell?"

"Then, there was this girl . . . ," Milton said.

"Hey! We don't want to hear any more," Charlie interrupted. "Just take a walk, pal."

46

God's Holy Bible University of Beachton, Alabama, ceased to exist when the state and regional accrediting bodies, as well as the office of the Attorney General and the Alabama State Police found much fault with it. Before this happened, Robert Fritata had graduated from God's Holy Bible College of Medicine and had completed his residency in Christian Psychiatry at Holy Blood Hospital, affiliated with the university and subsequently converted to a mushroom farm.

With such credentials as he had, Fritata's prospects for certification in ordinary practice were limited, and he found his way into the United States Army, where he was assigned the rank of captain, and practiced comparatively harmlessly for twenty years. Most of the soldiers placed in Fritata's care suffered from fairly commonplace disorders, covered in one of the two large compendia that made up his medical library—and he treated them with a degree of success comparable to that of other psychiatrists.

His only departure from standard technique was that of having disturbed patients handle poisonous snakes, but his conservative commanding officer ordered him to discontinue this avenue of treatment, even though it was popular on the wards.

After retiring from the army, Fritata bought a house, conveniently located between the East and West Arterials, and converted the living room to an office. He bought an ad in the telephone directory, which read, "Robert Fritata, M.D., specializing in the treatment of obesity."

Fritata had heard of a revolutionary method of treatment for the obese, and had gone at his own expense to Tijuana, Mexico, to attend a week-long training seminar conducted by Dr. Pierre Novatny, the visionary genius who had devised the method, achieved outstanding results, and had subsequently been all but stifled and destroyed by a jealous and shortsighted medical establishment in Europe and the Americas.

Fully trained by Dr. Novatny, whose regimen was so beautifully simple that a small paperback book of sixty-four pages could contain all the details of treatment, Fritata had every reason to expect a complete success in his new specialty. A month after hanging out his shingle, Fritata was seeing between thirty and forty patients a day, and had hired a receptionist, whom he also trained to administer injections.

The Novatny Method was based on the doctor's profound understanding of "cellular wisdom." Standing on the shoulders of earlier researchers, as scientists always do, Novatny had studied the practice of weight control through injections of human chorionic gonadotropin, a hormone extracted from the urine of pregnant women, a mode of treatment that enjoyed some success in the sixties. Coupled with a strict five-hundred-calorie diet, which was embarked upon for six weeks at a time, with daily injections, the results were highly satisfactory. However, a high incidence of heart attack, symptoms mimicking meningitis, kidney stones, mouth lesions, and dementia tended to prejudice patients against this approach, and after a few years, word-of-mouth caused a decline in the number of candidates.

Novatny had continued the hormone injections in his clinic in Mexico, long after most other practitioners had moved on to ear-stapling, balloons in the stomach, jaws wired or cemented shut, and labor-intensive and frustrating group therapy. However, while continuing to shoot patients up with HCG, which he manufactured himself, Novatny also ran an experiment in which he injected distilled water, but *told* the patients it was the powerful hormonal agent.

To his delight, the weight loss was identical, and the side effects were limited to those commonly associated with simple malnutrition. Novatny reasoned that the patients, believing they were being injected with the real stuff, had communicated this belief to their fat cells— which then behaved accordingly. In order to ensure that physicians he trained would not accidentally give the patients subtle cues that they were receiving a placebo, Novatny simply refrained from telling his students that the vials of Novatny's Specific, available only from him, contained nothing but aqua pura.

Robert Fritata's practice required twelve hundred vials per month at a cost of ten thousand dollars. The beauty of the scheme was that the shipments were labeled as distilled water, eliminating the complicated and expensive expedients usually attendant on international transport of experimental medicines.

Jennifer Gusdorf had to wait a month for her initial

appointment with Dr. Fritata. On the day, she sat in the crowded waiting room, filled out the forms handed to her by the receptionist, and read a small pamphlet and offset copies of several newspaper articles about Dr. Fritata and the Novatny Method she'd been given when she handed in her forms. By the time she was shown in to Fritata's consulting room, she had no more questions, and was eager to start her treatment.

Fritata was a handsome, open-faced man. He inspired confidence. "Ms. Gusdorf, you can expect to lose a pound a day for the first six weeks of your course of treatment. Then there will be six weeks during which you will receive no injections, and may eat anything you like. During this period, there will be a slight increase in weight—as much as twenty-five percent of what you had lost, which is normal. In your second six-week course of treatment, the weight loss will be less dramatic, perhaps a pound every other day. At the end of the second six weeks, we will need to conduct some tests, which we can do here in the office, and if all is going well—and I see no reason why it should not be—you may continue until you reach your goal. Is this satisfactory?"

It was entirely satisfactory.

"You will have to come every day, including Saturday and Sunday, for your injection. Cindy will work out a schedule for you. Miss one, and we have to wait three weeks and start all over from the beginning—so don't miss one." He twinkled at Jennifer. She smiled back.

"Now, I want you to eat like a pig for ten days."

"I beg your pardon?" This was not mentioned in the material she'd read in the waiting room. Dr. Fritata liked to save this part of the instructions for last.

"Yes, in order for this method to work, at the beginning

of each course of treatment, the patient is required to go on the biggest eating binge possible. Some people eat ten meals a day. Have milkshakes. Buy out a bakery. It's essential that you eat all you can—and the most fattening food you can find. This is to cause a feeling of surfeit and satisfaction that will communicate itself to the fat cells. It's very important. Do you think you can do this?"

Before she left the office, Jennifer phoned Milton and arranged to meet him right after work.

47

Milo was taking his time, it being the two P.M. to three P.M. lull. He picked up a news magazine, and read.

Michel Montignac, a Frenchman, having lost his job with an American drug company, lost thirty-five pounds, and at the same time read three hundred diet books. Having digested a fairly sizable portion of the available literature, he wrote one of his own, *Dine Out and Lose Weight,* which he published privately, and which sold five hundred thousand copies entirely by word-of-mouth, and without advertising.

This led to the publication of *Je Mange, Donc Je Maigris!* or, *I Eat, Therefore I Slim!,* and the establishment of La Galaxie Montignac, a multimillion-dollar-a-year enterprise including a vineyard, a chain of upscale food shops, Montignac chocolate, Montignac foie gras, a mail-order house, a quarterly magazine, a scientific institute affiliated with 350 physicians who prescribe his diet, and a company providing one-day seminars at four hundred dollars per participant.

Montignac also operates a deluxe restaurant, and organizes Caribbean cruises for "gastronomic dieters."

Montignac's method incorporates a strict regimen for several months, followed by a maintenance phase in which cheese, foi gras, chocolate, sausage, and wine are allowed.

Discounting calories as a "scientific swindle," Montignac measures foods by their "glycemic index," or the blood-sugar level they induce. He states that sugar stimulates the overproduction of insulin, which causes the body to store fat. Foods with a high index, such as potatoes and white bread, should not be combined with fats like butter. But cassoulet, a white-bean, duck, and sausage stew, and special fructose chocolate mousse are fine.

Milo flipped open his shirt-pocket notebook to a blank page, clicked his ballpoint, and wrote, "Consider writing diet book," wiped, flushed, fastened his trousers, washed his hands, and returned to his work station.

48

Francis Plumly, known as "Sis," had been thought to be a latter-day Shirley Temple, and had starred in two successful movies before it was discovered that he was a boy. This revelation was the top story in a number of weekly tabloids, and featured prominently on the television "soft news" programs that have largely replaced the regular newscasts, and even made the covers of *Time* and *Newsweek*, before interest declined and Plumly and his mother returned to normal—and for Francis, quasinormal, life. He retained the moppet curls that had formerly endeared him to the great public, and suffered through grade school and high school in Columbus, Ohio.

He also grew very fat, became chronically depressed, had no friends other than his mother, and seldom ventured out of the house. Francis and his mother never stopped thinking that someday he would achieve fame once again, and they made a thousand plans—none of which came anywhere near fruition.

Until Francis fanatically undertook to reduce. He starved and exercised with the fervor of a demented teenaged girl—which for all intents and purposes he was. He fasted for long periods, took terrible risks, bicycled frantically on a stationary machine, had his mother wrap his body mummy-like in plastic kitchen wrap to induce sweating, took amphetamines and suspect diet aids ordered from the back pages of magazines, and dreamed of liposuction and stomach stapling.

The result of his furious effort was a total normalization of his weight—which was then the only normal thing about him. His youth and robust constitution had permitted him to withstand his yearlong obsessive diet and self-torture binge without apparent harm. He looked cute. His depression lifted—inverted, in fact, and he became an intolerably cheerful and enthusiastic person, similar to little Sis Plumly, America's onetime almost-sweetheart—and he saw a way to get back into the public eye.

Francis became a diet-and-fitness guru deluxe. He began with appearances on the local news programs in Columbus, led inspirational meetings in various auditoriums around Ohio, wrote, and was the subject of, many articles in the Sunday supplements, and began to rake in money.

He had reasoned, correctly, that the make-or-break, blitzkrieg approach he had employed himself would not play well with the public, so he devised a weight-reduction program that ran along conventional lines, reduced food intake, and increased exercise—and positive self-image. Here, Plumly found within himself a mother lode of talent. He was great as a motivator. His special gift was conveying to the fat that he *cared*. Every one of his fans-cum-clients was made to feel that Francis Plumly, personally, was deeply involved, loving, rooting for them, thinking about them. His memory for names and details was prodigious. In the beginning he would send handwritten letters and make telephone calls to thousands of his charges. Later a platoon of secretaries and an electronic data bank took over—but he would still amaze his staff with his recall of seemingly everybody who attended his seminars, ordered his books, bought his prepared foods, workout clothing, exercise equipment, tapes, CD's, videos, computer software, inspirational art, greaseless cookware, or stayed at his resort–health farms, participated in his cruises and tours, and visited his theme park in South Carolina. He appeared, for a time, on at least three television programs every week, and had starred in six hour-long specials, seen nationwide, and two made-for-TV movies. He made several attempts to acquire one of the television networks, and came close.

He controlled a fitness empire which made that of the Frenchman Montignac look like *merde.*

But, for a long time, no fresh tape of Francis Plumly was seen. He made no personal appearances. His saturation of the media had been so complete, and his products were so well-merchandised and popular, that his absence was not publicly questioned—for the moment. But there was grave concern among top management in the Plumly organization. And Francis himself well remembered the downfall of little Sis, at the hands of a voracious and insensitive press. He would have to make personal appearances again soon, or the huge edifice would crumble.

But he couldn't. Francis Plumly had put on weight.

He had put on a great deal of weight. Beginning with his first vacation in eight years, during which he ate like a pig on an island in the Caribbean, and continuing out of control for almost two years, Francis had distended incredibly. His increase was in increments of scores of pounds, his intake was frightening to behold. Those members of his organization who dared to speak to him about his binge-without-end were summarily deprived of income and security. His eyes were wild, his belly inconceivable, his appetite unquenchable, his subordinates fearful. No one knew how much he weighed, but it was surely between six and eight hundred pounds.

Plumly had ensconced himself on an island in the South Pacific. No one was to know he was there. He had his people put it about that the secluded and heavily guarded compound belonged to a certain movie star, long ago gone recluse, and in his day too classy to now be of interest to the viewers of the infotainment programs. The state of mind of the few top executives who knew, and guarded, his secret was comparable to that of the German General Staff during the bunker days in 1945. A couple of them cracked under the strain and were hustled to the island compound, where they recuperated, and ate with their principal.

A small cabal of Plumly executives, loyal to their chief but with an eye toward saving the enterprise, took their corporate future in their hands, and began a secret search. On a certain night, a private jet left New York for the island. On board were these executives, and a curly-headed and attractive young man who was the spit and image of Francis Plumly in his salad days.

49

Milo experienced commercial inspiration while riding the bus. He had been flipping through his pocket notebook, repository of ideas, and germs of ideas, for literary works.

Rework *The Brothers Karamazov* with a science-fiction theme. Lesbian detective—plenty of explicit sex. Inner life of dogs. Long novel about many generations of W.A.S.P. family. Horror novel—with gore. Portrait of sexually fascinating girl like Linda.

The real-life Linda was out of town. Rubinstein, their employer, was liberal in giving her time off to visit some ailing relative out of state. This gave Milo a chance to marshal his energies, and pay some attention to writing. In truth, when she was around, his creative juices tended to flow in another direction.

He came to the page he had inscribed "Consider writing diet book." Somewhere he had heard that diet books are published in the hundreds, and hardly ever fail to make money.

"Why the hell not?" Milo thought. "How hard could it be?"

When he got home, Milo paused only to give birdseed and fresh water to Marcel Proust, the scrawny parakeet, and sat down to work with his coat still on.

Within two hours, he had the bare bones of an indubitable success—*My Favorite Things Diet Book*. Milo, with less than rudimentary scientific knowledge, Milo, who had never taken off a pound or missed a meal, Milo, the aspiring novelist and hot-dog server, had created a weight-loss system he knew—that anybody would know—was worth a fortune, and would make millions of dieters happy.

It was based on something he remembered saying to Milton, the editor. He had characterized it as one of "those" diets—but it had really been his own idea. It was elusively simple, obvious even, once someone had thought of it—and Milo was that someone.

It was based on one unsophisticated precept: Eat what you like. Milo made a note for a subtitle, *Eat What You Like—Be as Thin as You Want.*

In honor of his moment of inspiration, Milo first cited the Pizza-and-Chocolate-Cupcake Diet.

"Let's suppose that your favorite foods are pizza and chocolate cupcakes. There isn't a day when you wouldn't enjoy eating them. You love pizza, and you love chocolate cupcakes. If the pizza is great, you love it. If it's only fair, you still enjoy it. If it's lousy pizza—you'll eat it anyway. And you're the same way about cupcakes. You've loved them since you were a kid. You love to eat the chocolate icing first, and then the crumbly cake. Mmmmm! Sounds good, doesn't it?"

Milo was delighted to observe that he had a fantastic style for this sort of thing.

"You probably thought if you went on a diet, you'd never get within sniffing distance of pizza or chocolate cupcakes again, right?

"Wrong, dieter! On the My Favorite Things Diet, you can eat all you want of pizza of any kind, and all the scrummy chocolate cupcakes your heart desires! Sound impossible? It's not!

"There are only two rules to this revolutionary system of weight loss—and only two. If you will agree to obey these two easy-to-follow rules, you will have the same success as the thousands and thousands of people who have lost literally millions of pounds on the My Favorite Things Diet.

"Rule Number One: You must choose two, and only two, of your favorite things. They can be pizza and chocolate cupcakes (the author's personal all-time faves), cheeseburgers and french fries, bacon and eggs, fried chicken and apple pie, quails' tongues and Stilton cheese—it doesn't matter. You *will* lose weight.

"Rule Number Two: You must agree that, having chosen two favorite foods, you will eat them—and *nothing else*—for a period of thirty days. The first week will be heaven—and you probably won't lose any weight—but even if you adore bagels and chopped chicken liver, by the second week, you'll feel like eating a little less of them, by the third week less, and by the fourth week, even less. The weight loss is automatic.

"At the end of the month, what if you haven't reached your goal? It's simple—pick two other favorite foods, and do it all over again. Or, if you're not tired of your original choices, just keep going. I did the pizza and chocolate cupcakes for three whole months."

Milo went on to note a number of sample combinations, salami-and-potatoes, herring-and-doughnuts, clam chowder-and-milkshakes, et cetera.

He also dealt with questions of nutritional health, (take a multivitamin and eat an apple or a pear twice a week), and suggestions for the single person, the working person, kosher, Muslim, Hindu, vegetarian persons, alcoholics (he allowed beer as a food, but not spirits or wine), and sketched a design for a rotating cardboard food-combiner to be included with the book.

The proposal, including samples of text, an informal outline, various lists, and the sketches for the rotating device and a proposed cover, he put into an envelope, and prepared to address it.

But to whom? Milo phoned Phyllis, his mother.

"Hi, Ma? It's me. Quick question. Who's the biggest publisher of diet books these days? No, I'm not going on a diet—don't worry. I'm eating fine, Ma. I get four free meals at work. No, this is a project. Wait, I have to grab a pencil. Plumly-Worldwide-Knopf? They're the biggest? OK, Ma. I love you, too."

Milo's envelope was deposited at the post office the next day. It was delivered to Plumly-Worldwide-Knopf in New York City, logged in, seen and commented on by a first reader, handed to an editorial assistant, and snatched out of the routine manuscript progression by the editor-in-chief, vice-president, and publisher, who was about to take a long airplane ride, and wanted something work-related to be seen reading in the presence of his colleagues.

50

It was dawning on Milton, slowly, that the realm of the dead was even less a comfortable place to be than he had thought. The disarray of simultaneous past, present, and future and provisional past, present, and future had begun to smooth out and settle down into one continuum, which he was able to contemplate all at once, rather than as haphazard fragments. Thus Milton was starting to be aware of not only who he was, and had been, but who he might have been, had he done otherwise, and, worse, who he would be, when next given the chance. He was getting to know himself and, naturally, not liking it.

That this was probably true of everybody else was small comfort. Milton now understood the preoccupied and distant manner of the other inanimate inmates. They hesitated to respond to one another, or initiate more than the most superficial contact, because they were in various states of comprehending what shits they had been, were, and were likely to be.

Those who showed the slightest sign of kindness or compassion tended to win at Bardo and be reincarnated—if that was really what happened to them. Angela Podgorny, who had always been relatively nice to him, had drawn a winning card recently, and was beginning a new life in Philadelphia, circa 1904—an example of countersequential regeneration that put an unexpected spin on the transmigrational ball. Milton wondered if it was not out of the question to reincarnate as one's own ancestor, or oneself—if these things occurred randomly, which everyone seemed to think they did.

Milton thought it was probably random as well since, as far as he could tell from scuttlebutt garnered from old residents, a newly assigned soul had no memory of what had gone before and was unable to benefit from whatever insight it may have enjoyed between embodiments.

He had discussed this briefly with Charlie, who expressed the opinion that one's stay in the establishment he appeared to run single-handed was a reward, or a vacation between stints in the world of the living. But Charlie was an idiot, and knew—if anything—less than the humans. The only reason Milton had asked him was that Charlie was willing to talk to him.

It was a lousy system, Milton thought, and just the sort of thing God would be likely to come up with. Milton was conceiving a blasphemous aversion to the Deity, based on His frequent appearances on the stage of the casino. It was the same routine, word for word, every time—and stale from in the beginning, most of the jokes appearing to have been stolen from Bob Hope or some other professional comedian. Milton wouldn't have put it past Him to have created this cut-rate nirvana just to secure an audience.

"What we should have here," Milton had told Charlie, "is some kind of program. Counseling. Prelife therapy.

Help for us to deal with what has to be a taxing and confusing situation."

"We have the Teatime T-group, from which you are barred, by the way, until further notice," Charlie responded. "However, your comments are noted, and I will pass them on to management."

"Really?"

"Of course not. If you're bored, why don't you take up golf? I can get you into a foursome this afternoon."

As Milton's luck would have it, this conversation took place on a Sunday, and one of the players in his party turned out to be the Supreme Being.

How the game went for the nondivine players need not be recounted.

51

In the Bandag meeting room, Laszlo Gegenschein was enjoying a social evening with an old friend, the insane Wiley Sinclair. Each of the old men sat on a folding chair. On a third was a small black-and-white television set. They passed a large bag of cajun corn chips back and forth between them, and each had a liter bottle of grape soda beside his chair.

They were viewing a pseudo-news program, featuring a story in which a team of reporters were padded and made up to appear fat, and went about ordinary business, shopping in stores, eating in a restaurant, getting from place to place, recorded by a concealed camera. The reporters were alternately shown doing the exact same things dressed in their normal, fashionable clothing, and displaying their well-conditioned television reporters' physiques.

When appearing as themselves, the reporters received usual courtesy. Waiters took their orders, clerks in stores waited on them attentively, they entered buses and taxi-cabs, and received no special attention from people in the street. However, when cleverly disguised as fat people, they were ignored at sales counters, found it difficult to get the attention of waiters, and were passed by buses, and had their hails ignored by taxi drivers. Moreover, they were stared at and subjected to ribald comments from their fellow pedestrians.

The voice-over commentary was jocular. "Now let's see how Fattie Pattie and Rotund Rob fare in the same restaurant," the announcer said. "Look at the expression on the waiter's face! He'd better get some help! These two dinosaurs look *hungry!* Oh-oh! Wave to him, Rob—he doesn't see you! (How can he miss these two mastodons?) That's right, Pattie, wave your napkin! Help! Help! We're starving! We haven't had a bite to eat in . . . minutes!"

The old men were enjoying the show. "Look at the ass they strapped on her!" Gegenschein chortled. "It's like a horse's ass!"

"Personally, I like a big rump on a woman," Wiley Sinclair said. "Shows character."

The announcer went on, "Now our pudgy pair is trying to flag a cab. Here comes one! Wave him down, Rotund Rob! Whoosh! Gave our tubby twosome the go-by! Well, can you blame him? This couple could be hard on the springs—and I don't just mean in a taxi. Oh, this is too much! They're trying to hitchhike! Show some leg, Pattie—maybe you can get a ride in a meat truck! Oh! Look at the expression on this guy's face! He thinks it's the invasion of lard-butts from space!"

At the end of the segment, the reporters, in normal garb, were shown in the studio with the hosts of the program.

"Great piece, Pattie and Rob. Tell me, what was it like wearing those incredibly clever fat suits?"

"They were hot, Frank," Pattie giggled.

"Yes, they were," Rob added. "By the end of the day, Pattie here smelled like a genuine fat lady."

"I guess you know all about how fat ladies smell." Pattie twinkled impishly.

"Ho, ho, ho," Frank roared.

"I mean . . . how I guess a fat lady would smell," Rob stammered, flushed with embarrassment, but still charming.

General laughter from the studio crew.

"They always put on a good show, those 'News Now' people," Laszlo Gegenschein said. "You want to watch something else?"

"I'd better go home and work on the Blint manuscript," Wiley Sinclair said. "I'm going to submit it to a publisher soon."

Gegenschein switched off the set. "Did you tell me you do business with an outfit called Harlan Ellison, or something of the kind?"

"Harlon House. There's a editor over there keeps trying to buy something from me."

"That's the name. Someone left a package here, addressed to them. I keep forgetting to take it to the post office."

"Give it to me. I'm in there two, three times a week, negotiating. I'll take it by hand."

Seeing his friend to the door, Gegenschein reached into his cubicle, obtained a thick manila envelope, and handed it to his friend.

"Feels like a manuscript," Sinclair said.

"Whatever. Thanks."

Dear Milo—

Here's the manuscript I told you about. Just give it a read, and write a couple of pages summing it up. Of course, feel free to add a paragraph or two expressing your opinions.

The fee we offer is an insulting $50. But what the hell, that's show biz, ha ha.

Best,
Milton

Milo had received a very large, thick, but floppy brown-paper parcel. It looked and felt a little like a failed pillow, or a sack of seed. When he opened it, it looked like road kill—a tattered stack of pages of different sizes, small scraps of paper taped to larger ones, newspaper clippings, and yellow Post-it tabs protruding around the perimeter of the grayish jumble. An extra-thick giant rubber band held the whole thing together, and on top was Milton's typed note, on a clean sheet of paper.

Milo put the object in the middle of his table, and snipped the rubber band. The bird's nest of paper expanded, and seemed to breathe. He sat down and studied it. He felt as though he ought to be wearing rubber gloves. He dug into it at various points—it was far too irregular to riffle the pages with a thumb—and saw that much of it was in soft pencil, on lined notebook paper. Other parts had been typed on some badly abused typewriter, the open parts of the o's and e's were solid black, and letters appeared above and below the line. It had a vague aroma of fried fat.

There was a title page, of sorts:

THE DEVILS OF BLINT
by
Col. Wiley Sinclair, M.B.E.

Milo read:

3 May. Bistritz.—Left Munich at 8:35 p.m. on 1st May, arriving at Vienna early next morning; should have arrived at 6:46, but train was an hour late. Budapest seems a wonderful place, from the glimpse which I got of it from the train and the little I could walk through the streets. I feared to go very far from the station, as we had arrived late and would start as near the correct time as possible. The impression I had was that we were leaving the West and entering the East; the most Western of splendid bridges over the Danube, which is here of noble width and depth, took us among the traditions of Turkish rule.

We left in pretty good time, and came after nightfall to Klausenburgh. Here I stopped for the night at the Hotel Royale. I had for dinner, or rather supper, a chicken done up some way with red pepper, which was very good but thirsty. (*Mem.,* get recipe for Momma.) I asked the waiter, and he said it was called "paprika hendl," and that, as it was a national dish, I should be able to get it anywhere along the Carpathians. I found my smattering of German very useful here; indeed, I don't know how I should be able to get on without it.

Having had some time at my disposal when in London, I had visited the British Museum, and made search among the books and maps in the library regarding Transylvania; it had struck me that this might be of some importance in dealing with a nobleman of that country. I find that the district he named is in the extreme east of the country, just on the borders of three states, Transylvania, Moldavia, and Bukovina, in the midst of the Carpathian mountains; one of the wildest and least known portions of Europe. I was not able to light on any map or work giving the exact locality of the Castle Kramarchykowicz, as there are no maps of this country as yet to compare with our own Geodesic Survey maps; but I found that Bistritz, the post town named by Count Kramarchykowicz, is a fairly well-known place. I shall enter here some of my notes, as they may refresh my memory when I talk over my travels with Momma.

In the population of Transylvania there are four distinct nationalities: Saxons in the south, and mixed with them the Wallachs, who are the descendants of the Dacians; Magyars in the west, and Szekelys in the east and north. I am going among the latter, who claim to be descended from Attila and the Huns.

This may be so, for when the Magyars conquered the country in the eleventh century they found the Huns settled in it. I read that every known superstition in the world is gathered into the horseshoe of the Carpathians, as if it were the centre of some sort of imaginative whirlpool; if so my stay may be very interesting. (*Mem.,* I must ask the Count all about them.)

I did not sleep well, though my bed was comfortable enough, for I had all sorts of queer dreams. There was a bird—I was later told it was a variety of budgerigar—chattering all night under my window, which may have had something to do with it; or it may have been the paprika, for I had to drink up all the water in my carafe, and was still thirsty. Towards morning I slept and was wakened by the continuous knocking at my door, so I guess I must have been sleeping soundly then. I had for breakfast more paprika, and a sort of porridge of maize flour which they said was "mamaliga," and egg-plant stuffed with forcemeat, a very excellent dish, which they call "impletata." (*Mem.,* get recipe for this also.) I had to hurry breakfast, for the train started a little before eight, or rather it ought to have done so, for after rushing to the station at 7:30 I had to sit in the carriage for more than an hour before we began to move. It seems to me that the further East you go the more unpunctual are the trains. What ought they to be in China?

All day long we seemed to dawdle through a country which was full of beauty of every kind. Sometimes we saw little towns or castles on the top of steep hills such as we see in old missals; sometimes we ran by rivers and streams which seemed from the wide stony margin on each side of them to be subject to great floods. It takes a lot of water, and running strong, to sweep the outside edge of a river clear. At every station there were groups of

people, sometimes crowds, and in all sorts of attire. Some of
them were just like the peasants I saw coming through France
and Germany, with short jackets and round hats and home-made
trousers; but others were very picturesque. The women looked
pretty, except when you got near them. They had all full white
sleeves of some kind or other, and most of them had big belts with
a lot of strips of something fluttering from them like the dresses in
a ballet, but of course there were petticoats under them. The
strangest figures we saw were the Slovaks, who were more bar-
barian than the rest, with their big cowboy hats, great baggy
dirty-white trousers, white linen shirts, and enormous heavy
leather belts, nearly a foot wide, all studded over with brass
nails. They wore high boots, with their trousers tucked into
them, and had long black hair and heavy black moustaches.
They are very picturesque, but do not look prepossessing. On
the stage they would be set down at once as some old Oriental
band of brigands. They are, however, I am told, very harmless
and rather wanting in natural self-assertion.

It was on the dark side of twilight when we got to Bistritz,
which is a very interesting old place. Being practically on the
frontier—for the Borgo Pass leads from it into Bukovina—it has
had a very stormy existence, and it certainly shows marks of it.
Fifty years ago a series of great fires took place, which made terrible havoc on five separate occasions. At the very beginning of the
seventeenth century it underwent a siege of three weeks and lost
13,000 people, the casualties of war proper being assisted by
famine and disease.

Count Kramarchykowicz had directed me to go to the Golden
Krone Hotel, which I found, to my great delight, to be thor-
oughly old-fashioned, for of course I wanted to see all I could of

the ways of the country. I was evidently expected, for when I got near the door I faced a cheery-looking elderly woman in the usual peasant dress—white undergarment with long double apron, front, and back, of coloured stuff fitting almost too tight for modesty. When I came close she bowed, and said, "The Herr American?" "Yes," I said, "Wiley Sinclair." She smiled, and gave some message to an elderly man in white shirt-sleeves, who had followed her to the door. He went, but immediately returned with a letter:—"My Friend,—Welcome to the Carpathians. I am anxiously expecting you. Sleep well to-night. At three tomorrow the diligence will start for Bukovina; a place on it is kept for you. At the Borgo Pass my carriage will await you and will bring you to me. I trust that your journey from London has been a happy one, and that you will enjoy your stay in my beautiful land.

"Your friend,

"Kramarchykowicz."

4 May.—I found that my landlord had got a letter from the Count, directing him to secure the best place on the coach for me; but on making inquiries as to details he seemed somewhat reticent, and pretended that he could not understand my German. This could not be true, because up to then he had understood it perfectly; at least, he answered my questions exactly as if he did. He and his wife, the old lady who had received me, looked at each other in a frightened sort of way. He mumbled out that the money had been sent in a letter, and that was all he knew. When I asked him if he knew Count Kramarchykowicz, and could tell me anything of his castle, both he and his wife crossed themselves, and, saying that they knew nothing at all, simply refused to speak further. It was so near the time of starting that I had no time to

ask any one else, for it was all very mysterious and not by any means comforting.

Just before I was leaving, the old lady came up to my room and said in a very hysterical way:

"Must you go? Oh! young Herr, must you go?" She was in such an excited state that she seemed to have lost her grip of what German she knew, and mixed it all up with some other language which I did not know at all. I was just able to follow her by asking many questions. When I told her that I must go at once, and that I was engaged on important business, she asked again:

"Do you know what day it is?" I answered that it was the fourth of May. She shook her head as she said again:

"Oh, yes! I know that, I know that! but do you know what day it is?" On my saying that I did not understand, she went on:

"It is the eve of St. George's Day. Do you not know that to-night, when the clock strikes midnight, all the evil things in the world will have full sway? Do you know where you are going, and what you are going to?" She was in such evident distress that I tried to comfort her, but without effect. Finally she went down on her knees and implored me not to go; at least to wait a day or two before starting. It was all very ridiculous but I did not feel comfortable. However, there was business to be done, and I could allow nothing to interfere with it. I therefore tried to raise her up, and said, as gravely as I could, that I thanked her, but my duty was imperative, and that I must go. She then rose and dried her eyes, and taking a crucifix from her neck offered it to me. I did not know what to do, for, as a member of the Bandag Spiritual Fellowship, I have been taught to regard such things as in some measure idolatrous, and yet it seemed so ungracious to refuse an old lady meaning so well and in such a state of mind. She saw, I suppose, the doubt in my face, for she put the rosary round my neck, and said, "For your mother's sake," and went out of the room.

53

Milo made a note. "Starts off really well. The style is a little old-fashioned and creaky—but I think I like that. Keep feeling I've read this before."

At this point, the narrative ended abruptly, and Milo moved into illegible scrawls and smudges, supermarket coupons for canned goods, glued to pages, and articles, clipped out of an actual encyclopedia, presumably from some public library.

He learned that

Transylvania is a hilly region in northwestern Romania, enclosed on the east by the Carpathian Mountains and Transylvanian Alps and on the west by the Bihor Mountains. The main cities are Cluj, Brasov, and Sibiu, but the population is mostly rural and agricultural.

———

Budgerigars that escaped from domestication have apparently established breeding populations in Florida. The monk, or green parakeet, *Myiopsitta monachus,* native to southern South America, is among the hardiest of the parrot family. Permanent breeding populations are present in the region around New York City and are believed to have originated from escaped birds. Monk parakeets grow to about 11 inches long, and are green above, gray below, with dark blue feathers in the tail. They feed on fruit and grain and build large stick nests that may house up to 6 pairs of birds.

Added in pencil was a note: "Also in the environs of Blint. I have seen these."

Erich Von Däniken, writer, Swiss, b. April 14, 1935, has attracted public interest with controversial theory that extraterrestrial visitors communicated their knowledge to primitive humans in ancient times, thus laying the groundwork for the evolution of society and culture.

Harry Ford Sinclair, American, b. July 6, 1876. U.S. oil producer who founded the firm that bore his name. Went into oil business in 1901. Key participant in Teapot Dome scandal of 1923; acquitted of bribery charges, but later served a 9-month prison sentence for contempt of court and of Congress, in 1927.

In European folklore, a werewolf is a man who at night transforms himself or is transformed into a wolf (a process called lycanthropy) and roams in search of human victims to devour. The werewolf must return to human form at daybreak by shedding his wolf's skin and hiding it. If it is found and destroyed, the werewolf dies. A werewolf who is wounded immediately reverts to his human form and can be detected by the corresponding wound on his body. Similar creatures exist in folklore all over the world: the tiger, boar, hyena, crocodile, and even cat are were-animals in areas where wolves are not found.

Now Milo found a number of pages simply cut from the middle of newspaper pages, and trimmed to $8^1/_2 \times 11$, without regard to content, columns sliced lengthwise, or with top or bottom missing.

Then, what appeared to be a sort of children's story.

A NOTE TO THE READER

This is a factual story about Wereakeets. There are two things you need to know about Wereakeets to understand this story. First, the Wereakeet, or Budglodash, is a creature, formerly human, nightly transformed to a bloodsucking bird, a kind of vampire budgie, with powerful beak, and tiny little fangs. Second, anyone who is bitten by a Wereakeet will turn into a Wereakeet him- or herself.

The following is an account of events which took place in the village of Blint, Transylvania/Bukovina during the month of October in a certain year:

OCTOBER 8

A Wereakeet bought a house in Blint. We don't know where he came from—possibly the nearby village of Nornish. After he had unpacked his things, and looked at the newspaper, the Wereakeet went out and bit a citizen named Jonas Makrekscu outside an all-night doughnut shop. Mr. Makrekscu was annoyed.

The next day, Mr. Makrekscu turned into a Wereakeet.

Doughnuts originated in Transylvania/Bukovina.

OCTOBER 9

Wereakeets stay up all night and sleep in the daytime. Therefore, nothing happened on October 9th—until it got dark.

Then, Mr. Makrekscu, and the original Wereakeet, who may have come from Nornish, left their houses. The Wereakeet from out of town went back to the doughnut shop, and bit a woman— Grimna Farforshnik, a mother of six. Mr. Makrekscu bit a man who was sitting on his front porch.

Both of the bitten individuals turned into Wereakeets the next day.

OCTOBER 10

The following night, the four Wereakeets bit the entire police department of the village of Blint. (There were only four members of the police department, including the chief.) The police arrested the Wereakeets, but let them go the next day when they themselves turned into Wereakeets.

OCTOBER 11

The next night, the eight Wereakeets of Blint, including the four who had been the police department, went out in search of victims. They found them.

OCTOBER 12

Sixteen Wereakeets burst into the city hall, and bit the sixteen members of the Blint village council, which had met to discuss firing the police department for sleeping all day.

OCTOBER 13

The thirty-two Wereakeets of Blint went their separate ways and knocked on doors. They told householders they were college students earning their tuition by selling magazine subscriptions. Then they bit them.

OCTOBER 14

It was sixty-four Wereakeets who bought tickets to the movies. The film was *Dracula, The Movie, Part IV,* a classic. There was a good turnout. The Wereakeets enjoyed it, as did all but sixty-four members of the audience, who got fanged in the neck.

OCTOBER 15

The whole town attended the Midnight Madness sale at Onion King, a discount market in the outskirts of Blint. Many people got bargains, and in the parking lot, a hundred and twenty-eight shoppers got a nip on the jugular.

OCTOBER 16

Two hundred and fifty-six residents of Blint failed to show up for work. However, they did put on their best clothes and go out when night came.

OCTOBER 17

Five hundred and twelve Blintites felt like going out for a bite between 10 P.M. and dawn.

OCTOBER 18

When one thousand, twenty-four people had turned into Wereakeets, some of the people in the village began to suspect that something funny was going on.

OCTOBER 19

Many of those same people were up late, trying to find someone who wasn't already a Wereakeet. Two thousand forty-eight inhabitants said, "ouch," that night.

OCTOBER 20

Downtown Blint was now almost as busy after dark as it was during the day. Some of the restaurants remained open all night, serving coffee to those who wanted coffee. Four thousand ninety-six Wereakeets wanted something else.

OCTOBER 21

Eight thousand one hundred ninety-two Wereakeets did not pay their electric bills, brush their teeth, or put on clean underwear.

OCTOBER 22

Sixteen thousand three hundred eighty-four Wereakeets did not say please and thank you, kiss their mothers, or tidy their rooms.

OCTOBER 23

Thirty-two thousand seven hundred sixty-eight Wereakeets did not eat a balanced breakfast, get regular exercise, or go to bed early.

OCTOBER 24

Sixty-five thousand five hundred thirty-six Wereakeets . . . But wait! Only sixty-five thousand five hundred thirty-seven persons lived in Blint, including the Wereakeet who had moved from Nornish. There was only one inhabitant of the village who was *not* a Wereakeet. That was Levi Von Helsing, an amateur garlic fancier, who had always been somewhat unpopular.

On the night of October 24th, the entire population of Blint—except one—walked the streets, depressed. One Wereakeet tried biting a cat, but the results were unpleasant. Onion King stayed open all night and sold out all its bottles of ketchup, cherry soda, and strawberry toaster-tarts.

OCTOBER 25

The sixty-five thousand five hundred thirty-six Wereakeets left Blint. They left by train, bus, automobile, bicycle, horsecart, roller skates, and on foot. They headed for the nearby city of Blorsh. Most of the Wereakeets arrived after dark.

OCTOBER 26

On the morning of October 26th, there were one hundred thirty-one thousand seventy-two Wereakeets in the city of Blorsh. Half of them, being newcomers, slept in doorways, public parks, parked cars, schools, stores, on lawns, and in trees. Along about evening, they started to wake up.

OCTOBER 27

Two hundred sixty-two thousand one hundred forty-four.

OCTOBER 28

Five hundred twenty-four thousand two hundred eighty-eight.

OCTOBER 29

One million forty-eight thousand five hundred seventy-six Wereakeets. Blorsh had gotten too small for this number, and the one million forty-eight thousand five hundred seventy-six Wereakeets left for Farshningle, the provincial capital. Once again, the Wereakeets traveled in the daytime, and arrived about suppertime.

OCTOBER 30

And the next morning, there were two million ninety-seven thousand one hundred fifty-two Wereakeets living (so to speak) in Farshningle. The number of Wereakeets was about to approach the total population of Transylvania/Bukovina, and plans were under way for them to travel outside the country.

OCTOBER 31

We don't know what happened on October 31st.

ANOTHER NOTE TO THE READER

This true story of the Wereakeets of Transylvania/Bukovina describes the events of a little more than three weeks. Based on the rate of increase of Wereakeets, by the time you read this, everybody in the world—with the exception of Levi Van Helsing, of Blint, Transylvania/Bukovina—should have become a Wereakeet, or soon will. By my calculation, if the reader is not already a Wereakeet, he or she can expect to be bitten within the next five minutes.

Best wishes, and good luck from the author, whose real name is Jonas Makrekscu.

Milo made a note, "Charming, but I'm not sure what it has to do with the rest of the book so far. And why all the clippings and junk? Is there something I'm not getting?"

One of the things that Milo Levi-Nathan was not getting, and could hardly have been expected to get, was that Levi Von Helsing was his own ancestor, and that Jonas Makrekscu, another historical personage, researched by the lunatic Wiley Sinclair, figured in the descent of his irascible stepfather, Felix MacGregor.

In his cage, Marcel Proust gnawed on his cuttlebone and gazed lovingly on his master.

54

Milton decided that no one was going to help him, neither God, angelic being, nor man, alive or dead. If he simply allowed himself to be carried along on the currents and eddies of causation, if that's what it was, or karma, he would be consigned to who knew how many lives of comparative sameness, without direction or progress toward a goal.

The thought of hapless authors who had padded through his office, while he lived, in their cheap crepe-soled canvas shoes from the dime store, crossed his mind. Like Milo, they lived in hope, never knowing how to make things happen for them, never knowing if a way to make things happen even existed. These poor bastards tried to play such hands as they had been dealt—and so had he. And he did now.

Well, no more! Milton had a mind, much clearer than it had ever been before. He had a body, in fact the same body he'd always had—and it appeared to function just the same in the realm he now inhabited, as when he'd had life. What was to keep him from initiating some program of genuine self-improvement, right now, right where he was?

Would taking himself in hand have an effect on possible subsequent incarnations? Who could say? But, he reasoned, it couldn't hurt. If management wasn't going to make a serious effort to offer needed programs for personal improvement, he would do it himself—and not just for himself. He would teach and encourage others, as he uncovered the way toward a better Milton.

Milton got hold of a piece of cardboard, and a felt marker. He made a sign, and posted it on the corkboard outside the dining room:

Deceased persons interested in joining a serious weight reduction and fitness program, meet today at 3:00 P.M. on the tennis courts.

He chose the tennis courts, because he anticipated a large turnout.

55

Milo puzzled over what appeared to be random notes, in thick pencil, mostly indecipherable. There were occasional passages he was able to make out, dealing with strange lights in the Blintish forest, unearthly visitors, and the word "vengeance," frequently inscribed in margins, heavily underlined. There was something fascinating about poring over this hodgepodge and palimpsest of a document. It was like trying to observe some inconceivable activity at night, at a distance, and through a dense thicket, similar to the time the four stewardesses had rented the house behind his. He felt a strange excitement, almost fear. He knew he would have to study these grimy pages over and over, in order to extract some clue to what it might all be about. It was a museum piece, this creased and crumpled opus, full of dead screed folds, holey galleys, and spiral glyphics. It played on his mind in flickering shadows.

Now Milo found a block of clean white pages, neatly

typed. He was drawn out of his deep deciphering slowly, like the house lights coming up after a play. The top sheet of the neat stack of twenty-pound, fifty percent rag bond, was sharply daisy-wheeled,

```
        THE DISKOUNTIKON
              by
```

Wiley Sinclair

It was his own outline! It scintillated beneath his desk lamp. Milo felt a slow, swirling confusion envelop him. For long moments, the apparition of his text suggested some proof of Eastern European magic, psittacine lycanthropes, visitors from other worlds. How possible? Why here, among scribbled ravings? Had Milton, the editor, accidentally included it in Sinclair's mare's nest of a manuscript? Was it a joke? Was this merely Milton's haphazard way of returning his outline to him? But why had his name been erased and replaced?

In the clear desk light, he saw the thin threads of rubber cement, his booby trap for negligent and dishonest publishers. They were intact along the edges of the paper. Not a page had ever been turned. Not even the plagiarist had bothered to read it.

Milo leaned back and let out a long breath. In his mind was a turmoil of thoughts, most of them murderous. Marcel Proust narrowed his eyes, and hissed softly in sympathy with his aggrieved master.

56

"So she says to me, 'Milton, I'm going to lose weight.' "

"People are always saying that," Alan Plotkin said, brushing corn muffin crumbs off his vest.

"She tells me about this method that gets fantastic results. You get these hormone injections—makes your body think it's pregnant. It's a well-known fact that pregnant women, even if they're undernourished, tend to produce healthy babies. Whatever nutrition there is goes to the fetus first. The injections, coupled with a low-calorie diet, bring about a fantastic fast weight loss."

"The Novatny Method," Plotkin said. "Used to be popular. Diagnosing the side effects from that one was almost a separate branch of medicine. I thought it was outlawed by the U.N."

"There's a Dr. Fritata right here in town, who's refined the technique. He gets great results," Milton said.

"Slippery Bob? He's still around? What a character!

The stories people tell about him are priceless. His refinements don't involve picking up rattlesnakes, by any chance?"

"I don't think so. Anyway, the first stage of the treatment is you have to eat all you can for ten days."

"Nice touch."

"Jennifer showed me all this literature. It made complete sense to me. There was plenty of science."

"Right. And as a scientist, you understood it all."

"Well, I'm an editor. That makes me a sort of generalist. I can understand what I read. Besides, I took plenty of science in high school. It's not as though I were an ignorant person."

"If I asked you to go somewhere for electroshock therapy would you be willing to go along with it?"

"You think I need it?"

"Yes, but they'd refuse to administer the voltage I'd prescribe. Go on with your story."

"Well, Jennifer was just about to begin her ten days of wild eating, and then go on the program."

"Let me guess . . . you decided to keep her company."

"Right."

"And maybe go for the injections yourself."

"Right."

"You'd see how it went."

"Yes."

"But this way, you'd be ready, having already done the binge part."

"Something like that."

"You said the all-out fressing goes on for ten days, and it's been a week since I saw you last—and you mentioned none of this—so I assume you're still in the midst of the big chow-down?"

"No. Something happened."

"Tell."

"Well it began . . . fairly sedately at Gypsy Bill's."

"The Evening in Budapest special?"

"We each had two."

"God."

"It went on from there. We ticked places off by nationality: Mexican, Chinese, Italian, Greek, Indian, German, Polish, West Indian, kosher. We quit going to work. We'd walk around, building up an appetite and planning, discussing, where we'd go next. That was for the first couple of days. Then we just sort of stayed in her place, ordering in and cooking. We went out to shop. We invented dream meals—then we made the dream come true. We took catnaps. We rented videos. It was real intimate."

"I'm imagining."

"I mean, both of us had done this sort of thing before, but never with another person. Jennifer said no one had ever seen her eat like that. I'd always done it in private myself. We bought ice cream by the gallon . . . gallons. We made a hundred potato pancakes and ate ninety of them. We stayed up all one night, baking cookies, making egg-malteds, and watching Brian Donleavy movies—the video store had a special rate on them."

"It sounds very *gemütlich*."

"We told each other things we'd never told another soul. We confessed our worst deeds, and our secret hopes. We slept in the same bed. We saw each other naked. I used her toothbrush, with her knowledge and permission. I shaved with the razor she uses on her legs. It was that intimate."

"And then what happened?"

"After a few days, she wanted to have sex."

"You weren't having sex?"

"Well. We were concentrating on eating. It didn't come up."

"So finally she had to think of it."

"Only thing . . ." Milton trailed off.

"Was?"

"I didn't want to."

"Well, that happens. Sometimes, after a little nap . . ."

"No, I didn't ever want to. I don't have those kind of feelings about her."

"Still, common politeness—you were staying in her house—in her bed, for pity's sake."

"I couldn't, Doc. She turns me off."

"I thought you liked her."

"I like her, but she turns me off sexually . . . because . . . she's fat."

"Putz. *You* turn you off sexually because you're fat. Why didn't you call my service—say it was an emergency? I'm almost afraid to ask this—you didn't tell her your reason, did you? You made some gentlemanly excuse, right?"

"Well, actually, we'd been so honest with each other. I was sort of in the habit of . . . saying what was on my mind."

Plotkin took a long breath. "Speaking as your psychotherapist, I have to tell you that you are a worthless, annoying, destructive shitbum. If you see this lady again, which I have no doubt you will, both being as dysfunctional as you are, give her my card. She's going to need to talk to somebody."

"So I was wrong to mention it?"

"I'd say so."

57

Milo found Wiley Sinclair's return address on the brown wrapping paper that had fallen to the floor. Milton had apparently pasted a new address label onto the package, sealed it up again, and had the mailroom stick new postage over the crazy quilt of mostly one- and two-cent stamps in the upper right-hand corner.

Sinclair lived in the Hermione, a residential hotel, one step up from a flophouse. Milo knew where it was, not far from Gypsy Bill's Hungarian-American Cafeteria and Bakery.

Milo did not want to confront Milton right away. A suspicion was dimly materializing. Could it be that Milton, Milo's one literary friend, his one connection with the domain of letters, his gateway to the career he knew to be his destiny, was a creepy shit? There were questions he wanted Milton to answer, but he wanted more information first.

He shoved the clutter of pages into a paper shopping bag from Circumferus Maximus, and set off in the direction of the Hermione.

58

Milton was sitting in the wood-paneled office of Dr. Silon, his regular physician. Dr. Silon had been the Cramer family doctor, and had taken care of Milton all his life. He had battled his way through medical school during the Depression, and through the South Pacific during the Second World War. He had practiced as a neighborhood family doctor for almost fifty years. Now he was at the end of his career. He'd been bored almost the whole time.

"You were a fat baby," the gnome-like old healer was saying. "You were a fat kid, growing up. Now you're a fat man. In my opinion you were destined to be fat. What about it?"

"It's wrong to be fat."

"It's not wrong, and it's not right. It's what you are. A lot of my patients have been fat. Not many of them became something else. You're worried about your health? Your health's OK. I'd rather see you get a little more exercise, not smoke, eat plenty of vegetables, and avoid stress than try to diet. But that's not good enough for you, is it?"

"I should lose weight."

"Listen to you. You don't even say, 'I want to lose weight.' You say, 'I should lose weight.' What if I were to tell you that you *shouldn't* lose weight? What would you say then?"

"But I know I should lose weight. And as to wanting to lose weight, everybody wants to. That's all anybody talks about."

"Milton, I've known you all your life, and I can't say I've ever liked you very much. However, you are my patient. You're asking for advice, how to lose weight?"

"Yes."

"I could give you a diet. I must have given you fifty diets. They don't work. You tried psychotherapy?"

"Yes."

"That doesn't work. I suppose you've taken various pills."

"You prescribed them."

"They don't work. Diets from books don't work. Going to meetings doesn't work."

"There's a Dr. Fritata . . ."

"He's a schmuck. All he'll do is make you sick. No, Milton, none of those things work. I've used them all, sent patients to every quack—pretty much nobody lost weight, and nobody at all kept it off."

"So, in your opinion, there's nothing?"

"Opinion! I'm not talking about opinions! I'm talking about facts. After fifty years, almost, I guess you can say I've seen it all. Nothing, nothing has ever worked . . . except one thing."

"There is something?"

"Someone. There is someone. This is not for every-body."

"Someone who can help me?"

"There is one man who can help you—but only if you are motivated enough."

"I'm motivated plenty."

"It will cost you everything you own, and leave you in debt."

"I don't care."

"All right. Let me see if I can find the address and phone number."

The aged doctor clawed painfully at his box of index cards. Milton scarcely breathed.

"Here it is!" the old man said.

Milton paid the five-dollar consultation fee he'd paid for years, and left, clutching a page from Dr. Silon's pre-scription pad bearing the address and telephone number of Dr. Werner Unterwerfer of Potlatch, New York.

The old doctor sat back in the leather chair, now grown too large for him, and lit a cigarette. "What a shmendrick that boy is," he said to himself.

59

Had Francis Plumly set foot outside his compound, which included a house on the order of the Ringling mansion in Sarasota, and visited Lupowit City, the main habitation on the island of Lupowat in the South Pacific, he would have occasioned no end of praise and celebration on the part of the Lupowatians. This would have had nothing to do with his celebrity, wealth, or power. The simple islanders knew nothing of these. Plumly would have gladdened their hearts because at a weight within hail of a half-ton, he would have been the most beautiful manifestation of humanity they had ever seen. Fat is beautiful on Lupowat.

Plumly, however, wasn't going anywhere. He hardly moved out of his baronial bedroom or, except to use the reinforced commode just beside it, even his bed, much less his mansion. He held court with his subordinates, managed his worldwide commercial empire, read his mail, took his calls, and ate his many daily meals right where he was.

To the bedside came top-level executives, continental, zonal, and hemispheric managers of the vast Plumly enterprise. And here the former moppet, no less winsome and lovable for his hippopotamian hugeness, chaired a meeting of supreme importance to the survival of the organization.

Kevin Schuh, twenty-four years of age, an installer at the Long Island City, New York, branch of Hush Mufflers, a national chain of auto repair shops, had been spotted by an alert Plumly executive while replacing the exhaust system of a 1978 Plymouth Horizon. His resemblance to the younger, and thin, Francis Plumly was astonishing. Schuh had been approached, offered a substantial sum of money, a free dental makeover by one of the best practitioners in New York City, and the services of a team of the finest acting coaches anywhere. He had lived in Plumly's own Long Island mansion, viewed endless hours of tape of the great fitness guru in his salad days, and been drilled day and night by the fifteen coaches in speech, movement, details of personal history, preferences, and mannerisms, until, in an actual test, Plumly's own mother had not a clue that Schuh was anyone but her own son.

Now, Kevin was to be presented to Plumly himself. If their leader approved, he would assume the role of the public Plumly, making personal appearances, recording television spots, new exercise videos, testifying before congressional committees on fitness and health, and making well-publicized visits to inspire and encourage the morbidly obese.

Plumly had only been apprised of this scheme two days before the highest echelon made their trip to Lupowat, bringing Schuh with them. The executives were sweating and trembling. Plumly had never been compassionate—in fact, he was known for vindictiveness and cruelty—a subordinate who made a mistake would not only be dismissed, but usually ruined, and hounded to oblivion. Since becoming immobile, the diet despot had tightened the reins to a frightening degree. If Plumly did not like the Schuh idea, people would suffer.

It was an anticlimax. Schuh was presented, dressed in one of Plumly's own rhinestone-studded exercise costumes. The monumental media maven sized him up.

"The kid's cute," he said. "Looks exactly like me."

The executives held their breaths.

"Talk, kid," Plumly said.

"Do the routine about the Plumly Weight-loss Revolution," one of the executives whispered.

Schuh made an adorable face, and curtsied with one finger against his chin—exactly as Plumly had done to the delight of millions of TV viewers, time after time.

"*I love you all!*" Schuh squealed. "You don't have to be fat! *People!* We're going to start a revolution! We're all going to lose weight, and look great!"

Schuh stuck out his behind, and strutted up and down, petulantly, hands on hips, tossing his curls.

"That's enough," Plumly said.

There was a silence. A smell of sick sweat emanated from the executives. Schuh's, or Plumly's, sincere smile was frozen on Schuh's face.

"He's perfect," Plumly said. "Get the video people in here. Get me makeup."

In minutes, the resident camera crew was set up, Plumly

had been fitted with a dark wig and moustache, and had conferred briefly with young Kevin.

The lights went on, the cameras rolled, and Kevin, perfectly, executed a Francis Plumly inspirational visit to a profoundly overweight sufferer—with Francis Plumly in the role of sufferer. Plumly's name in the scene was Melvyn Killebrew.

(Melvyn in his bed. He's holding a rosary.)
MELVYN
Heavenly Father, give me a break. I've tried to lose weight, but I just get fatter and fatter.
(Francis enters.)
FRANCIS
Oh! Look at this poor baby! Melvyn, you got so fat you can hardly move! Isn't this sad?
(Close up, Melvyn)
MELVYN
Francis Plumly! Oh, my God! Francis Plumly! Oh, God!
(Close up, Francis)
FRANCIS
Yes, Melvyn! It's me, Francis! I'm here to help you!
(Close up, Francis, crying, smiling)
MELVYN
Oh, God! Oh, God! Oh, God!
(Two shot)
FRANCIS
Now, Melvyn, I'm not going to lie to you—because I love you. It's going to take a lot of work, but we're going to take *all* that weight off you.
MELVYN
Oh, God! Oh, God! Oh, God! Oh, God!
FRANCIS
I'm not going to *let* you be fat! Do you hear me, Melvyn?
MELVYN
Oh, God! Yes, Francis! Oh, God! Oh, God! Oh, God!

FRANCIS

And we're going to start *right now! Right now,* you hear me, Melvyn? We're going to get you out of that nasty, sloppy bed, and up on your little feet, and dancing. *Right now! Right now!* Give me your little hand, dear.

(Wide shot, Francis helps Melvyn up)

FRANCIS

That's right, Melvyn! You can do it. Slip on your tiny slippers. And, a-one, and a-two! Come *on,* Melvyn!

(Sings. They dance)

You put your little foot in!

You put your little foot out!

You pick your little foot up, and shake it all about!

THAT'S RIGHT, MELVYN! YOU'RE DOING GREAT!

You do the hokey-pokey, and you turn yourself around!

That's what it's all about!

(Two shot. Melvyn collapses, Francis hugs him)

FRANCIS

You're *beautiful,* Melvyn! *Beautiful!*

MELVYN

Oh, God! Oh, God! Oh, God!

(Tight close up, Francis to camera)

FRANCIS

Melvyn is going to lose *all* his weight. And I'm going to help him. With the help of our Lord, Jesus Christ, Melvyn is going to hokey-pokey his way right down to the slender, beautiful person he was meant to be. And *that's* what the Plumly Weight-loss Revolution is all about.

"Cut! It's a wrap! We can use this one. Is Kevin all squared away with legal? Everything signed?"

"Everything is covered, F.P.," one of the executives said. All the executives were beaming.

Francis Plumly's hand shot out, and grabbed Kevin Schuh by his exercise shirt. He was drawn down on top of Plumly, who was again lying on his bed. Plumly pulled

Schuh's face down to his, until their noses were touching.

"Kevin, you talk, or fuck this up in any way, and I will have you killed—for sure. You got that?"

"Yes, sir."

"Good boy. Have a jelly doughnut."

60

Wiley Sinclair wasn't in when Milo arrived at the Hermione. The man behind the desk, in the predictably depressing little lobby, done up in Formica and bullet-proof glass, told him where Sinclair could be found.

"Bob's Jew-Boy," the desk clerk said. "Around the corner. It's kosher-style fast food. Sinclair hangs there a lot."

Milo remembered Bob's Jew-Boy from an earlier incarnation as El Pollo Loco. It had been two or three other things before that. Now it was a mock deli, with plastic salamis hanging behind the counter. The color scheme had been changed to Israeli white-and-blue and the plaster head with microphone mouth into which drive-in orders were addressed, having been a clown, a Mexican bandit, and a chicken, was now painted to resemble David Ben-Gurion.

The menu had never changed. What had been a Bandito Burger was now a Kibbutz Burger. Real deli-style pickle

bars and genuine Jewish-type mustard were the only offerings that had not also been available at El Pollo Loco. The
flagship sandwich was the Jew-Boy, of course. Two all-
beef patties and a processed potato pancake, on a bun tex-
tured to look like sliced rye bread.

The place was failing as had all its predecessors failed.
The location was bad. No prospects for franchises had
come forward, and the owners, a consortium of doctors,
including Robert Fritata, were sustaining a useful loss for
tax purposes.

Milo had been told to look for a man in a black raincoat with argyle socks. There were no customers in the
place at all. Milo decided to wait and have a snack.

He had a Jew-Boy, and then another. They were not
bad, in a synthetic sort of way. He was contemplating
ordering the special-of-the-month, the Yasser Arafat
Palestinian Potato Pocket, when someone who could only
have been Wiley Sinclair came in.

He was an old man, hair dyed red, wearing his black
raincoat and checked trousers which stopped well short of
his shoetops, exposing bony ankles in vivid argyles. He
had very thick glasses, and watery red-rimmed eyes. He
ordered a side of deli-style pickle bars, and a large black
coffee, and headed straight for Milo's bolted-down table.

"See this, Fatty?" Sinclair said, throwing a leg over the
bolted-down chair. "This was General Grant's lunch every
day in the field. Pickles and black coffee, and strong cigars. Also, more or less what the monks at Suizenjii
Monastery used to eat. Concentration food. Keep eating
those Jewburgers, and the fat will go straight to your cor-
tex."

"Mr. Sinclair?" Milo asked.

"That's my name, Fatty. Don't wear it out. What can I
do for you?"

Milo reached into his shopping bag and pulled out the mare's-nest manuscript. "I want to talk about this."

"What's that?" Sinclair asked, pointing a pickle bar.

"What's this? It's yours," Milo said.

"Never saw it before in my life."

"It's got your name right on it," Milo said.

"Give that here, Fatty." Sinclair clawed at the title page, and ran a horny fingernail under his name. "Ah yes, it's mine all right. What about it?"

Milo bent the truth a little. "I'm vice-president, publisher, and editor-in-chief at Harlon House Publishers. My name is Milton Cramer."

"I get it, you're here to negotiate. Well, listen, fella, you're talking to an attorney. I'm gonna write you a contract that will bring the tears to your eyes. You're not playing with kids here. Let's go to the bottom line. How much, Fatty? Don't dick me around."

"Ten thousand," Milo said.

"Done! It's a deal! Shake hands!" Sinclair grabbed Milo's hand in his claw, and pumped it. "You big fat sissy, you folded up like a baby. You're no match for me, didn't I tell you?"

"The paperwork will take a couple of days," Milo said. "We'll sign, and hand over your check sometime next week."

"I keep the movie rights," Sinclair said.

"Of course. Now, if you don't mind, I'd like to discuss the manuscript."

"Fire away, Fatty. You're paying the bill."

Milo dug his pristine outline out of the mixup of pages. "What's this?"

"I have no idea. What?"

"It was in with your manuscript."

"Let's have a look," Sinclair said. He dripped pickle

juice on the outline for Milo's science-fiction masterpiece. "Oh yes, that's part of my book."

"It's yours?"

"Sure."

"Liar! It's not! It's someone else's work! You stole it! It's plagiarism!"

"Plagiarism! Ha! I've got plenty worse things wrong with me than plagiarism! Besides, I didn't steal it—I found it."

"You found it?"

"Yes, somebody left it at my friend's place. A manuscript in a sealed mailing envelope. So I took it and put it in. It's an *objet trouvé*. I'm an avant-garde author. I believe in serendipity."

"But this is the work of another author!"

"So what? Everything comes from somewhere."

"You think you can just do whatever you want?"

"I can do whatever I want. I'm crazy."

He had a point. The old man was crazy as a bat. His role in the matter was incidental. Milo had found out what he wanted to know. Milton had somehow lost, or had never received, his manuscript, and had lied to him.

"So you have some pissy scruples, leave that part out," Sinclair said. "It's not important. What's important is that this book contains the most revolutionary revelations since Teapot Dome. Do you even realize, Mr. Fat Publisher, what you have here? Did you understand it? Do you know what this book is about?"

"No, not really," Milo said. "Tell me."

61

"I'd like to kill him. That son of a bitch," Jennifer Gusdorf said weakly. She'd fainted twice already in the course of twenty minutes.

"Ms. Gusdorf, I beg you, please take a little chicken soup. It won't harm you, I swear," Alan Plotkin said.

"But Dr. Fritata was very clear that if I went outside the prescribed five-hundred-calorie diet, the treatment could fail."

"What treatment? He's starving you to death—that's the treatment. You're a big girl, you can't live on a half bagel, a few slices of turkey breast, and a pickle. Trust me, this is not the way."

"But I've failed at everything else," Jennifer moaned.

Joe, the counterman, had brought her a cup of soup, and she sipped at it delicately.

"See?" Plotkin said. "Isn't that good? Don't you feel the strength coming back?"

"I do feel better." Jennifer smiled weakly. "But I'm shooting my diet all to hell."

"It's all right. I'm telling you this. I am a doctor. And unlike that piece of filth Fritata's, there are no spelling errors on my diploma. By the way, is he the son of a bitch you'd like to kill?"

"No, Milton."

"Oh, him. Except that it's in direct contravention of my oath, I'd like to kill him myself."

Jennifer brightened up, "He is a schmuck, isn't he?"

"That is my diagnosis, but I shouldn't discuss another patient with you. Now, promise me you won't go back to that quack."

"But I have to do something!" Jennifer wailed. "Look at me!"

"You're cute as a bug's ear," Plotkin said. "You make me want to violate my ethics."

"Really? If you want to violate, I could always change therapists."

"It's a possibility. But now, I want to talk to you about this weight-losing business."

"OK," Jennifer said, munching a saltine.

"Been trying to lose weight a long time?"

"Oh, years."

"And of course the weight came on over a period of time."

"Yes."

"So, without getting technical, why should you expect it to go away fast?"

"Because . . ."

"Yes? Think about it."

"Well, I *want* it to go away fast."

"Because?"

"Honestly? I think it's because I know I will only be able to stick with whatever diet or exercise plan for a certain amount of time, and I want to get maximum results before I get dumped on by a shit like Milton, or some other event distracts me, and I go out of control again."

"Whereupon you gain the weight back."

"Plus more."

"Which is normal and standard in way more than ninety percent of cases. Now, I do not hold that most people should bother to try to reduce at all—for a lot of reasons, not the least of which being that they can't—but if you were to try, wouldn't it make sense to do it as slowly as you got fat?"

"I suppose."

"Suppose this: What if you absolved yourself of any guilt or pressure, and just decided to try to get a little— mind you, a little—more exercise, and just cut out some— only some—of the really wild out-of-control eating? Would you lose some weight?"

"I guess."

"Just do that."

"And that way I'll wind up thin?"

"I doubt it, but you'll lose some weight, and you won't make yourself sick."

"I'll think about it. So, you really want to go out?"

62

The addition of Kevin Schuh to the Plumly organization had an energizing effect on Francis Plumly. Plumly made up as a succession of morbidly obese characters, male and female, and of various races, including Shimar Shin, in full beard and turban, Rabbi Mordecai Benzion (same beard), and Jellybelly Rastaman, a delightful West Indian. With Kevin, he made a series of inspiring videos, which played on world television to resounding response. Digitally altered photos showing each of the housebound individuals in successive stages of dwindling were flashed under the credits at the end of each presentation.

Plumly also directed the New Products Division to move on the weight-reducing chewing gum and the new line of outsized clothing. And from the highest level at Plumly-Worldwide-Knopf, his recently acquired publishing conglomerate, he had received a proposal for a new diet book with distinct possibilities.

63

Milo was sitting at a tiny table in Bob's Jew-Boy with Wiley Sinclair. Milo had bought them both milk shakes, chocolate for him, and artificial strawberry for Sinclair, who was drinking it messily.

"I usually go into a trance when I want to remember," Sinclair said. "This is channeling. You will hear the voice of my spirit guide, Cookie Mendoza, a sweet eleven-year-old girl of old Spanish California. You will also notice that my face subtly takes on the appearance of that of an eleven-year-old girl. Don't get scared. This is all perfectly normal, though very rare. You're lucky to see this."

Sinclair clapped a bony claw over his eyes, threw his head back, and went rigid. A half-minute went by. Then he began to speak in a piping little-girl voice.

"Hola, Señor. I am Cookie Mendoza, a sweet eleven-year-old girl of old Spanish California."

Sinclair was rolling his eyes wildly. "I see a dark forest. It is long ago in a remote part of Eastern Europe."

At this point his voice resumed its usual irritating gravelly quality. "Beings from another world have established a colony, and are dormant, going through some sort of evolutionary adaptation."

"Remarkable," Milo said. "I wrote an outline for a science-fiction story that's very similar!"

"Shut up!" Sinclair said. "This is fact—from the spirit world! The extraterrestrials have chosen this site because the local peasants are primitive to a shocking degree, and should be easily dominated when the time comes.

"For a long time, nothing happens. The aliens evolve, quietly, in the forest. They're in a pupal state, concealed in the great trees. The peons never go very far into the forest, afraid of lycanthropes, tending to cluster in their villages, the principal one of which is Blint. Time passes.

"One day, a pupal nuncio goes around telling the other interplanetaries that it's time for the next phase of their evolution to begin. Small humanoids emerge, and begin to acclimate to their new home.

"One day, a villager, seeking to trap wild parakeets, sights one of the aliens in the forest, reports the event to the elders of Blint, and according to tradition is beaten and ostracized for bearing potentially bad news.

"Years pass. There are occasional sightings and encounters with the strange forest inhabitants. The locals opine that they are evil spirits, werewolves, and devils, all of which have been common in the vicinity.

"Around 1880, Andar Kramarchykowicz, a well-known liability and embarrassment to the community, wanders in the forest while stinking drunk, confronts one of the beings, and discovers he is able to communicate with it.

"Kramarchykowicz reports that the beings are representatives of a society possessed of knowledge and technology surpassing anything so far achieved on Earth. He further tells his fellow villagers that the apparitions are blue-violet in color, small, and light in weight, not physically strong, have an unusual luminescence emanating from their abdomens, and are strangely appealing and pleasant.

"When asked to produce this remarkable creature, or lead the others to it, he is evasive. People speculate as to whether he is lying, or possibly has done some harm to the otherworldly visitor—but not in Kramarchykowicz's presence, as he is known to be pugnacious and volatile, and inclined to inflict harm.

"There is much discussion among the simple people about the possible nature of the beings in the forest. Some believe they have come to lead and deliver them from the wretched conditions they endure. Others believe they constitute a danger, and should be eradicated, or at least chased away.

"Some attach a spiritual significance to the presence of the beings, and go looking for them with religious impedimenta, and singing prayers of thanks.

"Others, notably Kramarchykowicz and his family, go looking for them with other purposes in mind. In time, it is suspected that the Kramarchykowiczes are eating them.

"Some of the Blintites argue that it is all right to eat the extraterrestrials because they are not human.

"Others hold the opinion that it is not all right to eat them because they come from an advanced civilization.

"Some of the primitive apostate Jews of Blint argue that it is not all right to eat them, because they have toes, and are therefore not kosher.

"While others argue that it's OK to eat them as long as you don't eat the toes.

"The discussion rages back and forth. The Christian community is divided, as are the Jews. Of the two priests, the one who had led prayerful processions to the forest enjoins his flock to refrain from eating the heliotrope visitors, on pain of excommunication. The other takes the position that anything found in the woods was put there for Man to enjoy.

"Meanwhile, Kramarchykowicz and like-minded citizens are making a sizable dent in the population of alien beings. Some Blintians regard the consumption of sensate beings as tantamount to anthropophagy, and an outrage. Others claim it is nothing of the kind, and that the extraterrestrials are simply a fortuitous, and tasty, enhancement of the local diet.

"Local society splits along this line, and alien-eaters and non–alien-eaters begin to shun and hate one another.

"The actual question becomes moot after a while, as the little forest denizens become harder and harder to find. Finally none are found, and it appears that those Blinters inclined to do so have eaten all there were. The schism between those who partook and those who refrained, however, widens, and enmity hardens.

"Soon after, evil fortune beyond the usual crushing misery overtakes the people of Blint. Crops fail, wells dry up, tax collection and conscription befall them, there are fires, and more than the usual number of half-wits and monstrosities are born. The abstinent faction blames the purple people eaters, and especially Kramarchykowicz, for bringing punishment upon them all.

"There are outrages and retaliation. Blood oaths are taken. Families swear eternal enmity to other families. Arson becomes common, and there are assassinations, including the ancient Blintish ritual of 'flying vengeance,' in which specially trained parakeets are employed as weapons of death.

"Kramarchykowicz flees to the forest. His son, Bela, decamps at night, before a mob lays torch to his house. Certain Blintners swear their sons and their sons' sons yet unborn to harry, torment, and destroy Kramarchykowicz and the seed of Kramarchykowicz to the last of his line."

Wiley Sinclair leapt from his chair, and spun around wildly, waving his arms, then collapsed into the chair again, and said, "Whoo! What did I say? Cookie, where did you go? This sort of thing really takes it out of me. Get me another milk shake, will you, Fatty? There's a good fellow."

"Hallo! Is dis the elephant?" Felix MacGregor was speaking on the phone. "Drop vhat you doing, and come here immediate. Don't give me det malarky, you walrus. Tell Rubinstein your stepfadder told you. Right now, imbecile, and don't stop for a snack."

MacGregor put down the instrument, and went to a bookcase wall at the end of his office. He tugged, and a section of shelves pivoted silently on ball bearings, revealing a small room, lined with cork and containing nothing but an antique humpbacked trunk.

The trunk had come with MacGregor from Europe, had been his father's and his grandfather's before him, and contained a number of articles the nature and utility of which would have mystified all but a sparse handful of people on earth—although Wiley Sinclair, who was at that moment in the public library, happily researching a monograph on the secret covenant between Navajo and Tibetan shamans in the eighteenth century, might have been able to make a few shrewd guesses.

65

The turnout at the tennis court meeting at three P.M. was larger than Milton had anticipated. It seemed everybody was there. They were waiting for him when he arrived, and they seemed quite excited.

"It's amazing," Milton thought, "that no one has thought of this before. These people are desperate to lose weight—and together, we can help one another do it. We can finally take control of our lives—anyway, our after-lives." Milton had worked out some thoughts along these lines and noted them on scraps of paper. After a few inspiring introductory remarks, he would guide and develop a discussion, in which as a group they would devise the method by which they would effect their physical transformation. Once this was done, Milton would take his place as an ordinary participant, deriving the same benefit as the others from that which he had set in motion, and modestly refusing offers to serve as permanent leader of the new movement.

The meeting did not go just as Milton had anticipated.

The attention of the unfashionable unalive was fixed on him, but not so much on hearing what he might have to say. The crowd was more interested in saying things to him—brief emphatic statements, one- and two-word sentences, and suggestions of things—many of them physical impossibilities—that various individuals felt they would like to see Milton do.

Milton had also considered, if there had turned out to be sufficient enthusiasm, possibly leading the group in a little light exercise by way of ending their first meeting on an aerobic high note. This came about. A brisk run through the grounds, with Milton leading, and the shouting shades following close behind, wound up with Milton bolting through the door of Charlie's office, and then bolting that.

Charlie was in the office, wearing his gray sweatsuit and whistle, his sneakered feet propped on his desk, reading *The Wall Street Journal,* tomorrow's edition.

"Milton, you've made history," Charlie said. "You're going to be the second person ever to get himself thrown out of this place."

66

"I'm desperate. You have to take me."

"It's not that simple. We have a waiting list. There are people on the verge of death who can't get in here."

"My doctor—Dr. Silon—says that Dr. Unterwerfer is the only person who can help me."

"That's very likely. Dr. Unterwerfer is wonderful. But I don't see how we can schedule you anytime this year."

"Please, please! You have to take me! Isn't there any way you can fit me in?"

"You know, this treatment is rather costly."

"My insurance?"

"Won't cover all of it. And there are expenses beyond medical costs—housing, educational materials, approved athletic equipment, meals."

"I have savings. I can borrow from relatives. The money won't be a problem."

"And, of course, no one at all is admitted until they've had an initial interview with Dr. Unterwerfer."

"Can you schedule me for one of those?"

"The cost of the interview is fifteen hundred dollars."

"Fine. Fine. That's fine."

"You know, Mr. Cramer . . . I really shouldn't do this . . . but one of our patients has . . . left us . . . unexpectedly."

"So there's a vacancy?"

"Please don't tell anybody I did this for you."

"Oh, no, no. I won't mention it to a soul."

"Can you be here tomorrow?"

"Tomorrow?"

"I can move things around a bit . . . yes, I can have you in to see Dr. Unterwerfer at six in the evening . . . if you can promise to be here by that time."

"I have to make arrangements. There's my job . . . my apartment."

"The next available opening is in eleven months."

"I'll do it. I'll be there tomorrow. This is confirmed, right?"

"Dr. Unterwerfer will see you at six. Please don't let anything prevent your timely arrival, as the fee is not refundable. Ordinarily we require payment in advance, but, as this is a special case, just bring payment in cash for the initial interview—and our business office will need to see a bank statement and a list of assets, in order to determine if you can stay the requisite period."

"How long is that?"

"We ask people to be prepared to stay four months. It's sometimes shorter—usually longer. Will that be a problem?"

"No. I'll be there tomorrow. And Miss . . . thank you."

67

"So, Helf-vit, you arrived alraddy."

"What's this about?" Milo asked his stepfather. "We were right in the middle of the afternoon snack panic."

"Dis is important," Felix MacGregor said. "The time has come you should fulfill your destiny."

"What?"

MacGregor produced a tiny instrument, carved of beech wood, and resembling a miniature Fijiian war club. With the rounded knob he tapped Milo's head, sharply and precisely, whereupon the younger man went rigid and seemingly catatonic.

"Now begins the ritual," MacGregor said. He took Milo by a finger, and led him into the secret room. From the old trunk, he took a greasy hooded cape, painted with odd figures, which he put on.

MacGregor raised his hands, "Son of Blint! I anoint you vit the ancient herring of your ancestors!" So saying, he smeared something impossibly nasty on Milo's brow.

"I place upon your shoulders the feddered garment!" MacGregor took a foul thing, like a poncho, from the trunk, and slipped it over the head of Milo, who continued standing rigid, staring at nothing, breathing shallowly.

"I give you the beak of Death!" Over Milo's nose, he placed a curved beak, made of cow's horn, and fastened it by tying a piece of twine around the back of Milo's head.

"The helmet of tvigs!" A pyramid-shaped device, woven of little sticks of beech, he put on Milo's head, and tied it under his chin with more twine.

"The belly of light!" Around Milo's middle went a wide leather belt, with the bottoms of three beer bottles worked into it.

"I give you the parakeet dagger!" Into Milo's hand he placed a huge rusty knife, the handle of which was crudely carved into the likeness of a parakeet.

"Don't lose any of dis stuff," MacGregor said. "Now comes the chent of the Paradlak, the Wereakeet." For half an hour, Macgregor walked around the stock-still Milo, nasally intoning in the antique Blintish dialect. Time stood still, and ran backward. In Milo's mind's ear, he heard the wind whistle in the beeches, the twittering of the parakeets, the burbling of the Blintner, the local stream, the thunder echoing from the Blintenberg, the local mountain. In his mind's nose, he smelled the smells of his ancestral village, mostly the villagers. In his mind's eye, he saw many strange and terrible things—and in his mind's mouth he tasted the foods of his forebears, beech porridge, mush, slurry, and holiday herring, brought overland by oxcart.

"Mine boy," MacGregor intoned, "visdom old as the mountain, old as the voods, resides in your Blintish blood.

It is your duty to carry out retribution, to bring punishment to the last of the Kramarchykowiczes. I don't hef to tell you vhat to do. Vhere to find him, you vill somehow alraddy know. The spirit of the destroyer parakeet vill guide you, and make strong your hand. You vill not remember the terrible t'ing you go to do. Go now, and do it. Fly, mine pretty, fly, fly!"

It is well known that a person under hypnosis (which would come fairly close to describing Milo's condition) cannot be made to do anything he would not be willing to do in a waking state, but some part of Milo already wanted to kill Milton because of the matter of the manuscript, the likelihood that somehow Milo's other offerings had been made accessible to the literary kleptomaniac, Wiley Sinclair, and the shitty letters Milton had sent him. So there was no conflict in him as, clad in the trappings of the were- or vampire-parakeet impersonator, and holding the parakeet dagger, he headed for the Trailways bus terminal.

68

"So what was done with that irritating putz?" one of the terminally inconvenienced asked another.

"Oh, him the Almighty Power hurled headlong flaming from th' ethereal sky with hideous ruin and combustion down to bottomless perdition, there to dwell in adamantine chains and penal fire."

"You can't say the jerk didn't deserve it. Did he have anything to say?"

" 'Is this the region, this the soil, the clime . . . , this the seat that we must change for Heav'n, this mournful gloom for that celestial light? Farewell happy fields where joy for ever dwells,' and that sort of thing."

"What a schmo."

"Yep."

69

Dr. Unterwerfer was everything Milton hoped he would be, and more. Dressed in riding breeches and boots, a soft shirt, and an expensive-looking hacking jacket, he glowed with health and vigor and seemed completely unaffected by age. He even had a monocle. He strode into the examining room, whacking his calf with a riding crop and eating a Snickers bar.

"*Ja.* Got here just in time, I see. Vell, you big lump of dough. If you don't die in zuh night, ve chust may save your life, how do you like zat idea, Mr. . . . ." He consulted his clipboard, "Cramerrr?"

"I hope so, Doctor," Milton mumbled. "I hope you can help me."

Unterwerfer leaned close to Milton, and puffed chocolate breath in his face. "I'll tell you a little secret, Mr. . . . Cramerrr. . . . You are not vorth saving. Fat people are low, stupid, dirty. Zey lie and cheat. Zey . . . I mean you

. . . are nature's rejects. Fat people are not supposed to live! And yet, it is my destiny to heal zem. It iss a special calling. It couldt haf been lepers. It couldt haf been neegers in zuh jungle. It zo happens I am zuh patron saint—maybe zuh Christ—for garbage like you, Mr. . . . Cramerrr."

"But . . . you can . . . help me?" Milton said.

Unterwerfer poked him with his riding crop. "*Ja.* Zhere is nussing special aboudt your case. Chust zuh garden variety vill-less slob, in an advanced state of morbid degeneration. Ve vill haf you oudt of danger in a veek or two, and zhen vill trim you down, and make you resemble a human being—but you vill not be vun. You vill still be dreck, Mr. . . . Cramerrr. You vill still be zuh fat mutant— chust you von't look like vun. Und, do you know how ve vill achieve zis minor miracle? Do you, Mr. . . . Cramerrr?"

"No, Doctor. How?" Milton asked.

Unterwerfer's face transfigured into a radiant smile. "Vis kindness, my boy. Vis love, und understanding, und kindness. Here. Haf a bite of my Snickers—it vill be your last." He stroked Milton's cheek.

Then he was gone. The interview had taken less than five minutes. Fifteen hundred dollars. But, Milton thought, God knew what the great healer had been able to ascertain about him in that time.

70

Linda had not been visiting a sick relative, of course. She had been making her soft, well-upholstered, pink-and-gold, fragrant, blue-eyed way to Green Bay, Wisconsin, via the Winged Wienie, the Osterreicher corporate jet. Once landed, she would proceed by limousine to the Metzger House, Green Bay's grandest hotel, and to a luxurious suite, belonging to the Osterreicher Company and reserved for her exclusive use.

Here Mr. Lawrence Osterreicher, the third generation of sausage Osterreichers and sole owner of the vast tube-steak empire, conducted a series of strenuous interviews with Linda. She was being considered for a position of some importance, and Mr. Osterreicher wanted to be familiar with her every aspect. Some of her aspects he familiarized himself with repeatedly. And yet, when she had gone away, he found he wanted to familiarize again.

When the interviews had first begun, Linda had nothing

more in mind than a chance to make a start in big-time hot-dog management, but when she saw how exhaustive were the conferences with the great culinary industrialist, she began to suspect that she was being considered for something much better. So she was not taken completely by surprise, when, instead of bearing her down to the bun-shaped bed in the suite first thing, as was his usual practice, Lawrence had them both driven to "Wurstina," the family plantation, to meet his mother.

Not long after, in the Red Hot Lounge, the exclusive bistro atop the Metzger House, Lawrence placed upon Linda's chubby and delectable digit a ring, cunningly fashioned in the shape of an antique wienie-whistle, and offered her all that he possessed.

And not long after that, at the very time he was riding a Trailways bus in a hierophantic daze, garbed in the ritual accouterments of a Blintish assassin, Milo's answering machine recorded a message of tender and affectionate farewell.

71

Milton was directed to the room that would be his home for the next few months. It was similar to a middle-grade motel unit, on the bottom floor, with a small concrete patio outside. The grounds of the Unterwerfer Clinic were campus-like, tidily landscaped with shrubs and trees, and crisscrossed with walking paths.

He had not seen any of his fellow patients except for a disheveled and depressed-looking fat girl, wearing portable stereo headphones, who had shuffled past him in the hall. He had been instructed to fast overnight, in preparation for medical tests the following day, and had been given a thick sheaf of documents: histories to be filled out, schedules and rules for residents, information about laundry facilities, parking, recreational opportunities, religious services.

It was like arriving at college, only this time he did not have an earnest roommate who was chairman of the student homosexual rights committee, and this time, he would not waste all his time playing bridge in the dormitory lounge, be sent home with failing grades, and ultimately obliged to take his degree from a fundamentalist college in Alabama, at which the required textbooks had color illustrations on every page.

It was a fresh start. The thousand-and-one deficiencies of his personality and existence could all be traced to the one central misfortune of his obesity, and here he would be set free of that agonizing burden. He would emerge from this temple of healing as a butterfly from its cocoon, splendid and beautiful. He would soar, to what heights he could barely imagine.

"The old life is over," Milton said, and went out onto his patio to breathe the night air, where he was assaulted by what he took to be an enormous bird.

72

Milo woke up in his apartment with a splitting headache and a vague feeling of horror. He was disoriented as to what day it was, and had a black taste in his mouth. He stank. He recognized the smell as similar to that of an exhausted parrot. If the date-window on his watch was correct, there were almost forty-eight hours for which he could not account. The last thing he could remember was assembling hot dogs at Rubinstein's. Could he have been asleep all this time?

"I must be sick," he said.

He shook his head slowly, and waited for the haze to clear. It did no such thing.

The phone rang. It was Rubinstein, his boss.

"I should be at work," Milo mumbled thickly. "I'm sorry, but I think I may not be well. Must have gotten hold of some bad food, or something."

"No, don't come in," Rubinstein said. "I spoke with

your stepfather. The job is over. You don't come in any-more."

"What? Excuse me, I'm sort of confused. I'm fired? What for? I don't get this."

"Ask Felix," Rubinstein said. "You don't work here. You never worked here. I'm sorry, I can't talk to you any-more. Just leave town, and good luck."

"Leave town?"

"Goodbye."

The tiny light on his answering machine was flashing. He played Linda's message. She was marrying Lawrence Osterreicher, and could never see him again. She would always think of him fondly, and remember him as a good friend and one of the greatest hot-dog men it had been her privilege to know.

This news might have had a greater impact on Milo, had he been feeling better. As it was, he felt the relief he always experienced when, under the weather or distract-ed, he learned that Linda would not be making immediate demands on his strength.

Milo phoned Felix MacGregor.

"Yeh, sounds like you got a touch of parrot fever, fet slob. Maybe a little trip you should take. I'll give you some moneh."

"What about my job? Why did you tell Rubinstein to fire me? Wait. You want to give me money?"

"Sure, you water buffalo. It vas a lousy job. Better you should do somptin literary. You'll leave Marcel Proust vit me, I'll give you a couple thousand dollars, you'll take a little ride on an airplane. Get out of town for a few months—you shouldn't worry."

"I'll call you back. I've got to take a hot shower and clear my head."

73

When Milton was expelled from the dwelling place of the
metabolically different, he was not, as he feared he would
be, transferred to a region of punishing flame. He was
simply cast out, and found himself, quite suddenly, more
or less where, and more or less when, he had been in life—
the old neighborhood. The frame he had inhabited, however, had been disposed of, and he wandered his old
haunts, a disembodied spirit.

Being bodiless had a nasty feeling to it. He experienced
sensations similar to, but greatly surpassing, nausea, cold,
loneliness, confusion, pain, and all kinds of hunger.

Milton's mind was an uproar of emotions, thoughts and
half-thoughts, oddments of memory, and instinctive
twitches. Sights and smells, fragmentary recollections, and
vagrant ideas assailed him in wild succession. He saw
incalculable numbers of people, places, and events, heard
everything. With no physical senses to filter stimuli, the

world in which he had once resided was an assault and a torture.

He tried to hold a single item in his attention, to focus. It was next to impossible. He had to find a refuge. He had to shelter from this storm of sensation. This was dangerous. He risked inhabiting the physical arrangement of a pile of dog shit, or a telephone solicitor. It was something like the process leading to rebirth Natalie had explained to him—but he wasn't remembering that.

There was Milo, taking a shower.

. . . there Leviathan
Hugest of living creatures, on the deep
Stretch'd like a promontory sleeps or swims,
And seems a moving land, and at his gills
Draws in, and at his trunk spouts out a sea.

Milton instantly knew what he had to do. He made a supreme effort. He concentrated such self as he had into a sort of astral lunge.

Milo, in his shower, suddenly felt that he was not alone. He experienced a momentary flashback to the apposite scene from the movie *Psycho*—only worse. This hallucination included Milton. Then he sank to the floor of the shower stall in a death-like swoon.

74

Having Milton inhabit his body was unpleasant for Milo, who had never even liked the idea of having a roommate. It was not as revolting as it might have been, through the agency of a kind of psychic compartmentalization which, most of the time, obscured for each of the coupled personalities the consciousness that the other was present.

A similar partition had already created itself within Milo to protect him from the knowledge of what he had done to Milton's former physical self—but enough information leaked past, taking the form of murky inexplicit guilt, that Milton felt an incomprehensible obligation to be nice to Milton, and tolerate him, insofar as he knew it was him, which he did not, really.

Milo was aware of a new and surprising frequency of reference to Milton, his inclinations, opinions, tastes, and point of view, as an element in his inner dialogue.

For his part, Milton felt an enlargement of his slob- and glutton-self, and a slight improvement of his prose style.

All decisions would be immensely complicated as the multiple facets of two personalities—even such personalities as possessed by the collective Milo-Milton—interfaced exponentially, and inner conflict was likely to be rigorous. Now when either Milo or Milton talked to himself he got answers.

And the new cumulative I.Q. was above average—a category of which the individual partners had fallen short.

Two heads are better than one.

The alignment of the circuitry had only taken a few minutes, while Milo's body had lain inert on the floor of the shower. When they arose, mind-melded, neither was all that much more confused or disoriented than before the merger had taken place.

And straightaway, the new reinforced intellect had something to respond to. The phone rang.

"Is this Mr. Milo Levi-Nathan?" the voice asked.

"Yes, we are," Milo-Milton responded.

"This is Randolph Schipperke. I am executive vice-president of Plumly-Worldwide-Knopf, and I'd like to know if I am speaking to the author of the My Favorite Things diet proposal?"

"Yes, you are," Milo-Milton said.

"Am I correct in assuming that you have not submitted this work to any other publisher?"

"No, we have not," Milo-Milton said.

"I'm going to skip right to the chase," Randolph Schipperke said. "I've just spoken to Mr. Plumly. He likes your idea." Here Randolph Schipperke paused to allow Milo-Milton to exclaim excitedly.

"Wow! Really?" Milo-Milton exclaimed excitedly.

"He likes it *very* much. This is what Mr. Plumly proposes: He would like you to come to his private headquarters—which, by the way, is on an island paradise in the Pacific. There you will write the book under his supervision. Francisbooks, a division of Plumly-Worldwide, will publish the book and the accompanying videos, kits, and so forth, under the authorship of Francis Plumly, and you will be credited as associate author. The compensation will be generous. Is this of interest to you?"

"It sounds just fine," Milo-Milton said.

"Mr. Plumly would like to invite you to fly out to Lupowat, to confer with him. Our legal staff and myself will be on the plane, and we can discuss details on the way. How soon can you be available?"

"We're ready right now."

"And of course, you may invite your agent, attorneys, wife, or loved ones to accompany you."

"There will just be the one of us," Milo-Milton said.

75

Jennifer was at the wheel of the powerful L7, doing a steady ninety-five, heading back to town after an exciting day at the track. The sunroof and all the windows were open, and the stereo was at full volume, playing Plotkin's recording of the 1938 Glyndebourne Festival *Cosí Fan Tutte*. She was wearing Plotkin's bowler hat.

Alan Plotkin himself was relaxing in the passenger seat, with a white paper bag of macadamia nut double chocolate-chip cookies, occasionally feeding a piece of one to Jennifer, who licked the chocolate off his fingers as she took the morsel.

"More!" Jennifer said.

"Not too many," Plotkin said. "You'll spoil your supper."

"More!"

"It's a special supper," Plotkin said. "I called ahead, and told Nathan Eng to prepare the Mei Ling Supreme Ultimate banquet for four."

"Oh? Who else is coming?"

"Nobody."

76

Every year, a certain number of patients at the Un-terwerfer Clinic succumbed to "profound complications of obesity," a term of art similar to "shot while trying to escape." One of these was little Guppy Palmer, whose electrolytes had gone out while she listened to the Schubert C Major Quintet on her Sony Walkman.

An old soul, she adjusted quickly to existence in the Last Resort, and was even able to remember her previous sojourns, and ask after friends.

"I remember you," Otto Von Hinten said. "Last time you were. . . ."

"Natalie."

"That's right. Nice to see you again."

"So whatever happened to that guy you were rooming with?"

"Milton? He tried to start a diet club or something. Pissed everybody off. He was cast out."

"Wow! Forever?"

"So it would seem."

"So harsh. It was the residents who cast him?"

"Yes, but they had the approval of El Supremo."

"Really?"

"Well, you know how sensitive He is about His weight problem."

About the Author

DANIEL PINKWATER is regarded by critics, educators, psychologists, and law enforcement agencies as the world's most influential writer of books for children and young adults. He receives thousands of letters yearly, written in crayon—some of them from children. Since 1987, he has been a regular commentator on National Public Radio's "All Things Considered," and two collections of his essays have been brought out to the delight of listeners who can read. He lives in Hyde Park, New York.

About the Type

This book was set in Sabon, a typeface designed by the well-known German typographer Jan Tschichold (1902–74). Sabon's design is based upon the original letter forms of Claude Garamond and was created specifically to be used for three sources: foundry type for hand composition, Linotype, and Monotype. Tschichold named his typeface for the famous Frankfurt typefounder Jacques Sabon, who died in 1580.